REVOLUTIONS

To my family

REVOLUTIONS

Lory Manrique-Hyland

SITRIC BOOKS

First published 2004 by
SITRIC BOOKS
62–63 Sitric Road, Arbour Hill,
Dublin 7, Ireland
www.sitric.com

A CIP record for this title is available from
The British Library.

1 3 5 7 9 10 8 6 4 2

ISBN 1 903305 13 6

Set in 12 on 15 pt Granjon
Printed by ßetaprint, Clonshaugh, Dublin

Cuba is a country where politics, magic and religion are neighboring provinces, sometimes without boundary lines.

Thomas Hugh

En Cuba Se Derramó

My grandmother Josefina spontaneously aborted the day she saw the goat. Abuela Josefina Anna Arnau de Castillo had come out onto the patio very early that morning, immediately after her breakfast: a shot of espresso and a cigarette. The sun was rising over the fields, making the sugar cane glow like aged gold. The horses neighed in their stables to the west. She wished she could go for a ride that day, but the doctor had forbidden it. Her Maltese, Chichi, was at her feet. She could see the laborers with their machetes coming to work in the distance. They crossed the dirt road in slow-moving groups of twos or threes, hats obscuring their dark faces from her view, machetes resting on their shoulders like baseball bats. She breathed deeply and thought of her mother.

When her gaze descended toward the entrance of the patio, she saw a large, white goat. Her heart leapt into her mouth. She drew a deep breath, reached back and grabbed hold of a wrought-iron chair. The goat was very forward: he stared at her, as if asking for money. Chichi barked. The goat bleated once, turned and left. Stunned, Josefina watched as he retreated through the yard, out onto the road and away.

She clutched her abdomen, pain radiating down through her thighs and up to her breast. She barely made it to the bathroom. She stayed in the bathroom for a long time, not responding to the knocks and pleas of her maid Consuelo to tell her what was wrong. Josefina got off of the toilet only to see the fetus floating in the murky water. It was a male—she could see his fingers.

According to her, pregnant women should never be near a goat. They hadn't owned goats, and she had supposed that there was nothing to fear; but the goat had wandered onto their property near Santa Clara. She had been in her fifth month, and had aborted three previous pregnancies.

I overheard this one afternoon when I was around nine years old. The neighborhood women were over for a canasta game, gathered in the kitchen around our oblong table. They had cafesitos in front of them and tapped the plastic-coated, Spanish-lace tablecloth with their long fingernails or the edges of their cards. They had pretty much abandoned the game even before my grandmother told the story. Our neighbor from across the street, Marielena Guzman, was gabbing about the station wagon she and her husband had just bought. The Guzmans, I remember, were Protestants. Sitting across from her was Gabriella Gonzalez, an arthritic who lived down the block. She was rubbing her fingers and trying to focus on Marielena's conversation.

Maria, Gladice and I had been playing with dolls in the living-room next to the kitchen. We were the granddaughters and grandnieces of the women in the kitchen, so our bonds with them were strong—stronger than those with our parents. Mothers and fathers in our part of Miami worked all day, sometimes all night, and during that time we were malleable flesh for our grandparents' Old World ideas. Our mothers and fathers accepted this, deferring to their more experienced relations. Age ruled in our homesteads, and old folks were the flame of Cuban memory that lit us all with longing and made us understand that we were not really Americans.

In front of me, the older, larger and more aggressive Maria dominated play. We were preparing for a Barbie Doll beauty pageant, combing their hair and picking outfits and wondering if boys had parts that looked like the Ken doll's. Maria, who had intimate knowledge of her brother's body gained mostly at bath time, assured us that they didn't. The game took its usual course; our dolls inferior to Maria's, though hers was completely bald—the hair had been singed off the previous week by her brother, the small but resourceful Antonio. A hush fell in the kitchen and my grandmother's low sexy voice began at the back of her throat with a rumble, then permeated the kitchen with its sweet sound of loss. I turned in their direction. Marielena had quieted down and Gabriella looked uncomfortable.

I put my doll down, went into the kitchen and sat at the table with the women. Gabriella put her twisted hand on my hair and smiled. Marielena, seated to the right of Josefina, shifted her considerable weight, concentrated mostly in her belly. She was uncomfortable with my presence at the meeting of what I much later dubbed The Old Cuban Lady Nostalgia Club. Canasta was merely their pretext for reminiscing. They spoke about Cuba in the present tense and imagined their little two-bedroom homes to be Santa Clara cattle ranches, many-acre estates, Marianao mansions or expensive Vedado apartments. I wasn't sent out of the room, however.

I looked at her closely. Abuela's large green eyes had the sharp, penetrating look she gave people when she wanted their undivided attention and all the emotional resources they could offer. Her hands, though liver-spotted and brown, retained their elegance and their long, strong fingernails. They played a bit in her thinning curly hair which she had recently dyed red, and smoothed the edges of her blue polyester blouse against her slim hips. I sat there with the knowledge that being there was a privilege, absorbed every molecule of scent, hair color, word and gesture. Abuela reached for a Kent and lit it, slow and deliberate, before sharing her story.

When she had finished the tale about the goat, Marielena pursed her lips and said, 'You are sure it was the goat, Josefina?'

Abuela, whose gaze had become fixed on some point beyond the kitchen walls, focused now on Marielena as if for the first time, 'Of course. Of course it was the goat. What else could it have been? Almost five months along, I was—five months! These miscarriages, they don't happen so easily that late. The goat—it was probably sent by someone. A worker.' Abuela tamped her cigarette out in the small, brown glass ashtray and immediately lit another. I wondered what particular spell a goat could put on a woman.

Gabriella smiled, 'Josefina—why would it have been a worker? What makes you so sure?'

Abuela exhaled a great waft of smoke and looked out the window behind my head, 'They were always jealous of the local land owners, why wouldn't they be? We had a big house, two American cars, and they … they had their bohíos, their machetes, some home-made rum—'

Marielena tested Abuela, 'They had enough children—why hex yours?'

But Abuela was never one for Marielena's kind of logic. Marielena's system was faulty. It didn't allow for the effects of rain on certain days of the year, animals that cross your path, the meaning of lightning, hats on beds, unopened boxes, words said in a certain order. Abuela surrounded herself with this information, and more, in order to be able to decipher the true meaning of events, words whispered by the neighbors, feelings she could see in your eyes, actions taken or not. She responded to Marielena with condescension in her voice, 'Because of who they are. And because of who we are. There are many reasons.'

'Who are they?' Everyone looked at me. I had spoken—that was not part of the deal.

Gabriella had the most sense, 'Go outside and play ... the three of you.'

'But I want to know the rest of the story ...'

'Go.'

I pouted and dragged myself out to the living-room. Maria and Gladice had moved on from Barbies and were staring out the window. I ran over and looked out.

The neighborhood boys were out in the middle of the road, standing around a sinkhole that had formed the week before. The police and Department of Sanitation had cordoned it off with yellow hazard tape. All the boys were staring down the hole. They were sitting on their bikes ... in fact, Maria's brother Antonio was sitting on my bike.

'Hey, Antonio's got my bike!'

Maria, Gladice and I ran to the door, swung it open and pounded down the front steps, across the lawn and out to the sinkhole in the road.

'Antonio, wha'cha doin' on my bike? Give it back ...'

'Fuck off, ugly.'

The boys all laughed. Maria, Gladice and I were not amused. Maria fought back, 'I'm going to tell Abuela that you said fuck.'

'You just said fuck, too. I'll tell her that.'

'Well … you said it first.'

This line of reasoning was getting us nowhere as far as the bike was concerned. To move things along, I interjected, 'Ok, ok … Antonio we won't tell, really we won't tell your Abuela … just get off my bike. You have a bike of your own …'

'Not anymore.'

Gladice piped up, 'Why not anymore?'

Antonio pointed down into the hole. The girls and I sidled up to the edge, careful to keep more than arm's length from any of the boys. We peered over the edge, holding onto each other's skirts for safety. Down at the bottom of a hole taller than my nine-year-old self, Antonio's Huffy bike was laying in a puddle of muck, under a dripping City of Miami water pipe.

Maria's jaw fell open. 'Oooooh … you are in so much trouble. You just got that bike for Christmas!' Antonio stuck his tongue out at her. I was getting impatient. Did he plan on tossing my bike down there, too? Gladice and I looked at each other. Maria and Antonio could argue all day long and I still hadn't gotten my bike back.

'I don't know what happened to your bike, Antonio, but can I please have my bike back? You don't want it. It's pink and has a flowery basket … can I have it, please?'

'No.'

'You're mean!' Gladice was sweet, but she could never do much to win games or arguments. At least she was on my side.

'Mamá is going to take the belt to you, Antonio,' Maria was giggling at the thought. Antonio was distracted for a moment, with the thought of the belting he was going to get I suppose, so acting on impulse, I grabbed Gladice's hand, and we gave him a shove off the bike. The girls helped me get the bike back up and on its feet. I hopped on and rode away as swiftly as possible, putting distance between him and me. At the corner, I stopped and looked back. Everyone was gathered looking down into the hole ... and there was no sign of Antonio.

That evening, I was at the table with a glass of chocolate milk and two Oreos, sitting in Abuela's usual chair next to the back door in the kitchen. She came into the house through the front door and walked straight through the living-room into the kitchen to join me. I was worried, wondering if she'd been speaking to Antonio and Maria's grandmother, Gabriella, down the street. I sat tensely for a moment until she spoke.

'Looks like he broke his arm. They're taking him to the hospital.' She eased herself into the pleather and chrome kitchen chair next to mine.

'Oh. That's too bad.' I stared at my milk, secretly happy.

'Yes.' She reached for the pack of Kents she always kept in the cut-glass bowl on the table. She ripped the shrink-wrap off, pulled a cigarette out and lit it, dragging on the tobacco with satisfaction. I drank the milk and watched smoke curl out of her mouth.

'You be careful now. Don't go too fast on that bicycle of yours. Just ride on the sidewalk or grass. No jumping rocks or ramps. I can't even believe they were all playing out there. By that hole.' She reached out and smacked the back of my head lightly, forcing Oreo out of my mouth. 'And you—you shouldn't have been out there with them. Stay away.'

I wiped my mouth and chin, 'Ok, but you told me to go out and play.'

'Play, not fight! If you're not careful, you know, if you drop your guard, things happen.' Her eyes were on her hands stretched before her, the diamond ring on her left ring finger shining in the evening light.

'Uh-huh.' After the slap, I wasn't sure if we were heading for a lecture or a story. I sipped my milk, waiting for her words to take shape.

'No running around. You've already been told to stay away from those boys. You hear me? Keep the boys to a minimum. There's a ratio.'

'Yes, ok. Ratio?'

'If there are more boys than girls playing,' Abuela waved her finger back and forth, cigarette smoke trailing behind, 'the game is not for you. Ok?'

'I think so …'

'Ok?'

I gave in to appease. 'Ok.'

'And there's a lesson in Antonio's broken arm, too.' She paused to smoke. I squirmed. 'You have to look out for more than what you can see. Not just rocks, but people. And not just people, but their wills.'

'What?'

She smiled and touched the bangs across my forehead with one finger. I relaxed. 'Yes. People's wills are the most dangerous thing on earth, revealing themselves when you least expect it, turning your life into strange shapes you'd never thought possible.' I was a little bit lost, but as usual I listened, absorbed. 'Remember what the goat did to me?'

'Yes. I remember the goat.' I was a little bit shy about remembering this for some reason, probably because it involved bathrooms and babies. I looked down into my empty glass, reading the dark brown dregs of powdered chocolate like tea-leaves. What would Abuela tell me now?

'Well … the goat was only the beginning … I lost my hair, too. All of it to the will of others.' She slammed one hand on the table, making me jump. I looked up at her hair, teased into a helmet, looking sturdy and eternal.

Then she told me a story, one I would later corroborate.

Josefina started losing all of her hair a few years after she had seen the goat. She would wake up in the mornings with clumps of hair on her pillow. She would comb her hair, and it would fall in drifts at her feet. At first she accepted this without surprise, never deviating from her habits.

She usually woke early with Abuelo Rogelio, and made him coffee and toast before he headed for the office. Despite the cook's objections, she would insist on making his breakfast herself and watching him eat it every morning.

After Rogelio left the house the day stretched before her, long and slow. Sometimes she would bicycle through Havana in the early mornings before it got too hot. She must have looked amazing riding around in brown leather pumps and shin-length skirts, a polka-dot scarf wrapped around her head and tied under her chin to keep the sun off of her scalp, large sunglasses accentuating scarlet lips. But she was a better walker than a bicyclist and ran into passers-by on more than one occasion. One month a picture of her lying on the pavement in the Parque Central with her bicycle behind her and on its side appeared in *Zig-Zag* magazine. In the picture Josefina is laughing at herself with a wide smile. Though it is an embarrassing moment, she looks gorgeous. A man's arm is in the picture, reaching out towards her to help her up. The man's face and body can only just be seen peeking in from the edge of the picture.

Abuela paused her storytelling for a moment to light a new

cigarette. Then she looked at me: 'When Rogelio saw that picture, that was it. No more bicycle. In public anyway.'

I was leaning my head in my hands. My elbows rested on the table, 'Then where did you ride it?'

'Well ... in the back yard for some exercise, or even just up and down the street in front of the house, I guess, but no further. Not into town or to the park.'

So her routine changed after that. She would go to the shops like El Encanto in the mornings by car. She couldn't drive, but Rogelio would send a driver from the Port of Havana office building to pick her up and take her where she wanted to go. She would be driven home in time to meet Rogelio for lunch at noon. After lunch, one or both of them would nap until two, then he'd get up to go back to the office until about eight.

She stopped talking again, not as enthusiastic about her story now as she had been when she started. She grew quiet and smoked.

I pried: 'But what about your hair? When did your hair go? When did it come back?'

'Bueno ...'

During the summer months of 1952 and into 1953 Rogelio had not been coming home for lunch as often as usual, and frequently rang to say he had a business appointment. When he didn't lunch at home, Josefina would sit alone at the dining-room table with food for two in front of her. She would eat her small portions slowly and quietly, chewing each morsel of tortilla or carne asada. She would fix a stare on the large English porcelain bowl in the center of the table while she ate, disconcerting Consuelo.

She still did this when I was a kid. She still ate that way. She did a lot that way. Her movements were meditations in form, her time alone at the kitchen table dreamily inhaling Kent after Kent a practice in Zen smoking. My movements were quick and short, sure to knock something over. I'd broken countless figurines and espresso cups with my frantic rushes at the kitchen table, the television set in the living-room, the back door in the kitchen that led to the yard. She would get me for that, too, with a knock on the head and an admonition to be careful.

As a kid in 1981 I thought Abuela's stares were deeply thoughtful. But back in Cuba, Consuelo found Josefina's meditative stares to be akin to some kind of santero's trance. Consuelo lived in the Vedado with the Castillos, and traveled with them when they visited Santa Clara. She was a small, attractive mulatta who served their meals, cleaned their houses and helped the cook.

Consuelo believed that the santero's trances were beneficial, soothsaying, life-giving, essential, but she thought Josefina's trances were due to evil or illness; anyway, Consuelo has told me that evil is the root of all illness. So Consuelo had taken to sneaking around the house, secretly positioning glasses of water and candlesticks held firmly with their own wax on broken kitchen plates, hoping to capture the evil affecting Josefina. These glasses, however, had to be very well hidden, or Josefina would find them and fire her. Josefina was a firm believer in Catholicism in its pure Roman form; anything that deviated from the sanctioned rituals of the Church was Satanism. She believed this despite the fact that she crossed herself and said a misericordia each time lightning struck, and had a singular aversion to goats and other animals that she made a point to avoid, fearing the worst if she couldn't. She had a variety of habits that she believed would ward off evil. She knocked on wood and had a stock of words and phrases for every occasion. But Consuelo knew that spirits don't stop at thresholds, and did her best.

I've talked a lot with Consuelo, whose face I've seen staring back at me not only from across a room, but from soft-focus photographs of the 1940s. She was very pretty as a young woman. As in many of those photos, her black hair floats above her head in a cloud of soft illusion, her heart-shaped face looks at the camera from a coy angle. Her lips are softly parted. Her beauty was of a totally different sort than Josefina's. Josefina was statuesque; Consuelo was a pixie. Josefina was a glamorous charmer, mysterious and sharp-edged; Consuelo was open, sweet, honest. Josefina was long, cat-like and ethereal. Consuelo was petite yet shapely, healthy and earthy. The only place they overlapped was in their imaginations, which were both overactive. Though both were sharp-witted and perceptive, they filtered their information through a sieve of superstition and religion.

Consuelo had been a palpable presence in my childhood home. Abuela Josefina had mentioned the name many times in her verbal meanderings through the past, but she didn't know where Consuelo was now. Through a lucky coincidence and a small bit of research, I found her address. I went to find her because she was another way for me to connect to my family, to my past, to the people in the stories that made me unique. Without these stories, without these people, I was no one. I was an American with no pedigree, a nonentity trying to make herself into a somebody. Consuelo was like a member of the family. She'd worked in the house and on the farm, slept there, ate there, talked to people, heard things. She was an invaluable resource.

I met Consuelo when I was about twenty-four. The first time I saw her she was on her front lawn bending over some weeds. She was smaller than I could have imagined, wearing a pair of black polyester shorts and a ruffled, red polyester blouse with no sleeves. Her stomach was a firm, protruding medicine ball, but her arms and legs were a fit, dark tan.

Consuelo's house was in Central Florida, in an area surrounded by orange groves and cattle pastures. I had taken a bus from Miami as far as the Greyhound station in Lakeland, and had then biked the rest of the way with a change of clothes and a bottle of water in my backpack. Once I got outside of Lakeland proper, I turned down a dirt road two miles up from the Shoney's on Route 4. I biked for a long while, wondering if I had misread or miswritten the directions that Consuelo had explained to me over the phone a few days earlier. Orange groves crowded either side of the road, quilting a hypnotic pattern of light and dark on the pavement. Temporarily enveloped in cool and darkness, I felt like I was tunneling towards salt. Eventually, to my left, the trees gave way to pasture. I couldn't see an animal anywhere, and had only been passed by one pick-up truck piled high with plastic barrels, and a Toyota filled with teenagers. The desolation became hot and oppressive. The summer and its humidity pasted my wavy black hair against my neck and sent rivers down my spine. Hidden even from myself was my nervousness. I used it to fire my legs and pedal faster, it made my mind work looking for her house, it took away my hunger and satisfied me with anticipation.

Finally, after a bend in the road, the orange groves to my right came to a sudden end with a fence and a sign. Now there were houses on either side of the road, set far apart on dried-up plots of weedy land. A few large trees offered shade. As I biked past house after house, looking for number

567, I could see a lake shimmering behind the houses, making promises I hoped it would keep.

After looking closely as 559, 561, 563 and 565 glided past, I rolled up with the last of my steam to 567. She was out front, bent over weeds growing amongst yellow pansies within a low, white wooden border. She pulled the weeds with quick, short strokes, an expert at yard work. She was around sixty, but moved like a thirty-year old. I stopped my bike in the road, got off, and started towards her, walking my bike along beside me. I was shaking.

Consuelo stopped pulling. She'd probably heard the metallic sound of the bicycle chain and the crunching of gravel under my sneakers. She stood upright and turned to squint at me, shading her eyes from the sun with her hand. I thought of my hair and the bike ride. I pulled the rubber band out of my ponytail and ran my fingers through it to remove the hair stuck to my neck and face. I wiped sweat from my forehead with my T-shirt sleeve and smiled.

She sung, 'Marysol.'

I felt relief.

She came towards me, leading with her stomach. I leaned down and kissed her cheek. She reached for my upper arm, where the skin started poking out of the sleeve. She squeezed just below my tattoo of rosemary, leaving white fingerprints in my olive skin. She weighed me with her eyes, trying to determine what kind of person I was. I looked into them, small, slanted and brown.

She made her decision, 'You're beautiful.' She patted my cheek with her hand. 'Come inside.'

I followed her up the gravel driveway. Next door, a long-haired man squatted, tinkering with a Harley. He smiled and waved at Consuelo, who waved back. Her aqua-colored house had paint peeling near the tile roof and around the corners. The flower border was hiding rust stains along the wall. I leaned my bicycle against the side of her house, next to the door. Out back, I could see a small wooden dock jutting out over the lake. I heard chickens and other birds, the barking of dogs, something scratching on wood. When she opened the door to her home, a cat ran out into the yard, and sat in the middle of the front lawn, squinting in the sun.

We entered a sparse living-room. There was an old couch with faded green upholstery. Above it was a large portrait of Jesus Christ wearing the Sacred Heart. There was a small corner shelf with a statuette of La Virgen de la Caridad del Cobre surveying the room from her perch. In front of the Virgin were an orange and a bottle of White Shoulders. Across from the couch was a large but old television set with wood paneling on a moveable plastic and chrome television cart. The floor was clean, but chipped, black and white tile. The room opened into the dining area where there was a wooden table and six chairs. The dining-room opened into the kitchen, which was small and dark with a stained ceiling. A pot of black beans simmered on the stove. None of the rooms had doorways; they all opened into each other without introduction or preamble. Neither of them had much to hide from the other. There was no air conditioning, but the windows were open and ceiling fans were turning. Through the French doors in the back, behind the dining table, breezes from the lake cooled the sweat on my arms and neck, making me a little chilly despite the 85° temperature.

Consuelo put a cafetera on the stove to boil. She lit a Merit and offered one to me as she sat down. I shook my head. I had my own. We were silent, dead silent, until she took the first step in the bizarre dance of Cuban conversation.

She wiped her hand over her face, and nodded behind her in the direction of the lake, 'Like the Sea of Galilee, no?'

I looked at the water outside. I could see people on the far shore standing on their beach, ankles in the water. I wasn't sure what she meant, but I was grateful for the beginning.

'I've never been there.'

'Yes, no, neither have I. I mean, like with hope and promise. The whole area is a kind of Promised Land. Cheap land, lots of fruit.'

I nodded, 'Oh … yeah. I see what you mean.' I was surprised at how good her English was, that we could speak in English. Her accent was heavy, but her vocabulary very good. Abuela Josefina could only speak in Spanish.

We eased ourselves slowly into a real conversation, step by step, slowly peeling off the layers time had sewed onto our skins. We had to stop at four o'clock because her favorite Venezuelan telenovela was on. I sat silently on the couch and watched it with her. Afterwards, we went out to the back yard and sat on the shaky wooden steps that led down to the lawn. On the porch behind us were cages of chickens and rabbits and parakeets. Consuelo kept them fairly clean, but the smell was still pungent. We rested in the bright summer evening, our conversation drifting on emotional waves. My tack was into the past, and I was unashamed about prying. I wanted to know why Abuela had lost her hair. I wasn't sure how she would respond. She was not a Miami Cuban: she may have lived in the present. I sipped the bottle of Beck's she'd opened for me and waited for her response.

'Why Josefina lost her hair, I don' know. Maybe nervios, maybe she piss' someone off, as they say.'

'Who would she have pissed off to lose her hair?'

'Elegua, Oshun … how should I know?'

'What was it like during that time? What was she like?'

'When I notice Josefina's thinning hair, I was worry for her. I really was.'

Josefina's once thick, wavy locks were reducing themselves to strands of fine black straw. And Josefina noticed Consuelo noticing her hair. One day, while meditatively chewing chunks of lime-drenched avocado salad, she looked up from the bowl and saw Consuelo staring at her head, a look of pity in her eyes and a grimace on her face as if it were Consuelo's hair falling out and not Josefina's.

'I could no help it. I didn' mean to have such an expression on my face, but mi niña, I was so young. I was much younger than you. Anyway, when Josefina saw me, she swallow' her avocado and get up from the table, pushing herself off of the lace tablecloth with those long, strong, white fingers of hers. I cannot forget them—they were perfect. Then she left the room, swaying like a drunk. She slammed the door to the bedroom. I crossed myself several times, because, Marysol, you never know. I put the plates on the silver tray that we used every day—not the really good one for guests—and took everything into the kitchen.'

That afternoon, Josefina started wearing scarves on her head. Rogelio arrived home in the evening, newspaper securely under his arm, to find Josefina with a bright red scarf wrapped around her head, playing solitaire at the card table in the living-room usually reserved for guests. She hypnotically, deliberately put each card down in its place, spade on heart, club on diamond, and did not greet Rogelio.

Rogelio stood in the doorway to the living-room, examining her. He paused there for a moment, trying to locate, I imagine, the woman he'd married in the morose and distant lady sitting in a faux Louis XV flipping cards on a lacquered table.

She had become thoroughly humorless and uncommunicative. She went through her days mechanically, hoping for rest at the end but getting none. She'd toss and turn at night until Rogelio sent her out of the room so that he could get some sleep. Then she would sit in the living-room, smoking cigarettes and listening to Havana at night.

He shuddered. Josefina never looked up, though he was but a few feet from her. He turned and left without greeting the stranger in the room behind him.

Later that week Josefina went completely bald. Before preparing Rogelio's coffee and toast, she looked in the mirror of the bathroom and was shocked to see that all of the baby-fine hair that had been struggling to maintain a foothold on her head was gone. It lay on the pillow behind her in the bedroom.

'Dios mío,' she whispered. The nearly inaudible utterance bounced off the mirror and struck Rogelio lightly in the ear. He exited the closet next to the bathroom with a tie dangling around his neck and looked in on Josefina.

'Josefina!' He put his hand to his mouth. '¿Qué paso?'

Josefina carefully passed her hand over her head, feeling peach fuzz. 'I have no idea.' She started to cry in front of the mirror, clutching the sink. She looked down at her hands and noticed that her long, red fingernails contrasted well with the white of the porcelain. She sobbed. Rogelio approached her and put his hands on her waist, but, I imagine now, it must have been like reaching a million miles into the distance.

'He felt nothing. I know that he felt nothing.' Abuela Josefina finished her Kent and smashed it into the ashtray, circling the stub, seeking out and destroying all the embers. She got up from the table and went to the refrigerator, then started rooting around for the makings of dinner. I still had my empty glass of chocolate milk in front of me. But the story was half done. Where was her hair?

'Tell me more.'

'More?' She took chicken parts, pimentos, onions, tomatoes and garlic out of the refrigerator. From the cabinet near the sink she took a can of tomato paste, olives and capers. She put a pot on the stove and poured olive oil into it.

'Yes, more.' I got up and filled my glass with water from the sink. I watched her as she chopped the garlic and the onions; the smells that gloved her hands permanently. 'What happened after you lost your hair? I mean ... you have hair on your head now—is it a wig, or did you grow it back?'

Abuela looked annoyed. 'I don't wear a wig ... it grew back.'

'When?' I sat down at the kitchen table and watched her bustle around the stove, rice cooker and cutting board.

'After I lost my hair, the doctor suggested that I go somewhere to relax.'

Josefina packed her bags and left her husband to go to the place of her birth near the shores of Oriente Province. This was also the province of Fidel's birth. They were the same age.

The journey to Oriente had taken more than a day, but when she got there she was happy. She stayed with her brother Ricardo; his large, talkative wife, Barbara; and their enormous son Orlando in the house where she'd grown up. It was now a household of well-fed bankers. They refused to feed Josefina anything less than too much. Barbara turned out to be a bore, but her intentions were good. This branch of the Arnau family talked at high decibels and made large gestures with their hands, often knocking things over—they were influenced, Josefina was sure, by Barbara's side of the family and not hers. Meal times were regular and attended by all, including, very often, neighbors and their children. Josefina had no time for sitting alone, looking and listening. She started feeling better.

She lay on the beach, warming herself day after day, until her hair started to return. It came in thick and black, as it had been in the best of times. Her green eyes regained their luster and her clothes filled out as she gained weight. Her mornings were occupied with baths. She read French authors she'd meant to read as a teen: Proust, Balzac, Flaubert (but no Zola). In the afternoons, she wandered the streets of Santiago de Cuba, memories rushing back. She wandered with more freedom than ever before.

Still chopping onions, she explained, 'Because as a child there I was rarely allowed to leave the house. Señoritas stayed at home. Women who walked the streets were of a different sort.'

So, as a child she had stayed in. Her Andalusian mother wanted Josefina's creamy white skin preserved. If she were to go outside, she might get dark. Josefina would sit at the window in the dining-room, looking out at the mountains in sunlight, wishing for escape. She would sometimes slip out to climb a tree, chase a cat, dig a hole—but she would inevitably be found, reprimanded, washed and dressed and find herself back on the inside, looking out and wishing.

A music teacher came regularly throughout her youth to teach her lessons on the piano, which she has since forgotten.

'And she was always hitting my fingers! Hitting my fingers! With a long ruler she'd made of an old tree in her father's yard. She had no upper lip. I hated her.' Abuela waved her knife over the chicken. I leaned back into my seat.

When she was a teen, Josefina went to a girls' boarding-school. There was movement in her childhood—change; but the movement was from interior to interior. She remembered different locations, different faces, different lessons and buildings, but she never remembered the movement, the journey, how she got from here to there. She remembered no sun. Her youth was one of drawing-rooms and dormitories.

Now, she saw her old town as if for the first time. She enjoyed sitting in the square in front of La Granda where she could look out on the mountains that fortified the city. Perhaps she made one too many visits to La Palinda for ice cream, but La Palinda was across from the Cíne Rialto, whose pink edifice and bright green sign tempted her to come inside many afternoons. There she could see American movies with stars like Irene Dunne and Gregory Peck. She liked Cary Grant, but was suspicious of his charm. Tyrone Power took her breath away. Rita Hayworth was her favorite though, because Josefina felt that she resembled Hayworth herself. She didn't resemble Rita Hayworth in the least, but that doesn't detract from the fact that Josefina Castillo had her own kind of cinematic sex appeal and charm. She was hyperconscious of her walk, which was straight-backed and slow. She held her head high and didn't look at the ground. She never wore any shoe without, at minimum, a two- or three-inch heel. At fifty-five she walked into a room, and assumed that all eyes would be fixed on her as she moved. They often were. She tried to teach me to walk the same way, and I made an effort. I acquired her kind of confidence and held my head high, but I still lack her skill with spiked heels.

She perfected her walk during her time in Santiago de

Cuba. With each new hair she gained confidence and the ability to stand up straighter. With each new day, she became a better version of herself—taller, she thought, stronger, with bigger breasts and longer legs. She could feel power welling up within her and pouring out through her eyes and fingers.

During her second week in Santiago de Cuba she decided to write a letter to Rogelio. She had barely spoken to him for months. She wasn't sure what to say, but she felt compelled to communicate with him. Her growing sense of strength encouraged her inclination.

This story was interrupted by the sound of the key in the lock. The door opened and my father, Juan, stood in the doorway—a long, slim shadow backlit by the street lamps that had just come on. The appearance of any male was enough to make Abuela stop talking. She prepared the pollo fricasé in silence.

Esos Que No Tienen Compasión

I found the letter Abuela had mentioned in Abuelo's closet a couple of weeks later. I shouldn't have been looking, I suppose, but the closet was one of my favorite places to be. First, I would pick some of Abuela's best clothes and put them on. Scarves on my head, bangles piled on my arm, silk slips pulled over jeans. Then, I would crawl in over the shoes and belts, surrounding myself with his suits and some of her long skirts and dresses, and pull the door shut behind me. The dark opened possibilities and promised me futures the daylight never could. I would sit, swaddled in total darkness, until discovered and forced to come out.

One day on my way into the closet I knocked over a black and gold shoebox filled with letters, pictures, bits of cloth and pressed flowers. They scattered over the shoes, memories looking for a home. I collected them and put them back into the box. I put the cover on and held the box in my hand, unable to put it back where it had been.

I crawled back out of the closet and dragged the box out behind me. I looked at some pictures wrapped in yellowing paper. There was the picture of Abuela cut out from *Zig-Zag* and in the same envelope one of her and a small-eyed man who I didn't recognize, smoking a pipe. In another, there was one of her and Abuelo looking much younger, standing arm in arm in front of a white, stucco house with palm trees and Baroque trim around the porch. Abuela was plump and smiling. Abuelo's seductive smile curled up one side of his smooth, tan face. His eyes looked sad. I turned the picture over and read, 'El Vedado, 1948'. I picked a letter from among many, and sat on the bed. I read this:

April 1953

Querido Rogelio,
Santiago de Cuba has changed. The beaches have lost a little of their luster, but the city has an even deeper beauty. The pace is slower and the afternoons seem to last longer. The light is purer. I don't miss Havana much right now, although I miss you, of course.

I feel better. My hair is growing back. Are you going to visit me?

Tu querida,
Josefina

Abuela walked into Abuelo's room and found me with the letter. I looked up at the doorway, her slim shape blocking the entrance, and wondered what she would do. But she wasn't angry that I was looking into their past. She actually smiled when she found me on the bed with the shoebox of memories at my feet. The past was her favorite place to be.

To introduce me to her past, every rusted, jeweled and bleeding inch of it, was her ideal. She came over to me and took the letter out of my hands and read it with me looking over her shoulder. My reading was very good, even in Spanish, and she didn't have to read it aloud. I only had to ask about 'lustre' and 'profunda' and, of course, about what and where Santiago de Cuba was. We sat together on the yellow bedspread and, more than read the letter, we looked at the letter: the creases and coffee stains; the soft, almost onion-skinned paper; the shape of the letters she could still form, but with a less steady hand. I asked why and when she'd written the note, and she told me that it was the first letter she'd written to Rogelio when she started to recover.

Josefina had sat at the desk in her room in Santiago de Cuba, reading and rereading her draft of this letter that was destined to be read again by both of us in about thirty years, wondering if she was saying the right thing, or if she was saying enough. She thought about her waning attraction for Rogelio and considered it to be a temporary feeling—a passing condition not unlike her baldness or her trances. She hoped at any moment to overcome it. She thought about Rogelio and tried to feel passion.

Rogelio, to her, was the sum total of his possessions; his personality could be described as a list of facts. Fifteen years older than Josefina, Rogelio had once been a dapper young man. He'd been educated in a private boys' school in Connecticut and in the Jesuit Belén in Havana. He'd attended Boston College. He was as privileged as privilege went in Cuba during the 1920s and '30s—which was farther certainly than the guajiros sleeping on dirt floors, but not as far as the American playboys who spent winters in Havana and screwed their way from Varadero to Vedado. Rogelio himself had wooed many with his dark, pomaded hair and his large, blue, puppy-dog eyes. He spent money freely. He had a big car. He could speak English. He'd met Josefina at the Tennis Club. Their house was in the Vedado section of Havana. They'd kept Josefina's family farm in Santa Clara as a retreat, and a working farm—a money-making family heir-loom. They had the small dog, Chichi, but no children. There was no subtlety about Rogelio. His only idiosyncrasy was his alcoholism.

After drafting the letter she immediately went out to post it. She dropped the letter into the mailbox in the center of Santiago, and after she let it slip through her fingers, she stood there with her hand on the small metal slot, closed her eyes and imagined Rogelio in Havana:

The letter would arrive at his office near the marina. Ocean liners, cargo ships and small pleasure boats would be discernable through his office window over the couch. It was April and the weather had to be perfect there now, no rain, no clouds, though soon it would be too hot. Josefina imag-ined that he would finger the slim envelope for a while before reaching for a letter opener and slitting the paper open. He would be pleased that his wife seemed to be recov-ering, pleased with her description of Santiago de Cuba and the request for him to visit. He would fold the letter and slip it back into the envelope, open the top drawer of his desk and slide it under papers and pens. He would call the trim and leggy secretary into his office and ask her to please send a box of candy—whatever kind she saw fit—to his wife in Santi-ago de Cuba. His dark-eyed secretary, Magali, would proba-bly smile wordlessly in her secret way and leave the office, Rogelio's eyes on her legs as she tapped out in her snakeskin pumps. After she left, Rogelio would lean back in his chair and maybe think about lunch. Josefina was quite familiar with this behavior, having witnessed it herself on more than one occasion.

Josefina got annoyed. Her fantasy was going all wrong. She opened her eyes. A man wearing a straw hat stood in front of the mailbox, letter in hand, 'Are you feeling alright?'

Josefina smiled, 'Yes, sorry. I just … remembered something.' She stepped away from the mailbox and headed back in the direction of her brother's house.

Later that week, Josefina opened the front door of her brother's house and accepted a box of Chocolates de La Habana from a deliveryman. There was no note attached, just a return address at the Port of Havana. He never got around to responding to her letter in writing.

Que Sirva De Ejemplo

I came in through the open front door one afternoon making lots of noise: banging my Hardy Boys lunch pail around, throwing my jacket on the floor and slamming the door. I saw Abuela in the kitchen, a cigarette dangling between her fingers, her eyes staring through the window at the neighbor's house. I could tell that she hadn't heard me. I put my things down on the kitchen table and looked at her eyes. She noticed me standing there after a minute or two. She reached her arm out slowly, put her hand on one messy black pigtail and pulled it gently. I leaned in for a kiss, and she pecked me on the cheek, but said nothing.

I asked, '¿Qué pasa?'

She smiled vaguely and shook her head, then looked out the window again.

I walked behind her and went for the cabinet with the chocolate-chip cookies. I couldn't reach the cabinet, and started climbing up on the counter—a move that I knew was strictly forbidden. Once on the counter top, I turned to look at her from my seat on the Formica. Abuela didn't react, didn't even turn to look at me. I grabbed the blue bag from the shelf and sat on the counter fishing cookies out and piling them on a napkin I found near the sink, eyeing her every now and then to see if there would be a reaction.

Without turning to look at me, Abuela said, 'Why don't you go watch a little television?'

I put the bag back on the shelf, hopped off the counter, and took my cookies into the living-room. I planted myself in front of the television set.

Abuelo Rogelio came home later, around seven. By the time he walked through the door, I was sick with sugar and stupid from hours of unsupervised television. He was carrying a copy of the evening *Diario* and the black lunch pail Abuela had packed for him that morning. I jumped up to greet him.

He kissed me and pressed me to himself, asking, '¿Cómo está mí niñita?' I hadn't responded before he looked up through the doorway and into the kitchen. I followed his gaze and saw Abuela in the same position she'd been in when I'd come home hours ago. I hadn't looked up from the television set since three o'clock.

He went into the kitchen to stand by his wife. He called her name. She didn't look up, just stared out the window. I became uninterested in the television, riveted now by the scene in the kitchen. Abuela had become a statue. Her discolored fingers clutched the cigarette, which had burned down to an ashen stub. Her eyes stared, fixed on the scene out the window, the neighbor's orange Volkswagen Beetle the center of the portrait.

Abuelo called her name again.

She didn't move.

I wandered into the kitchen and touched her hand, imagining it as it had been years ago in Cuba, strong alabaster.

I looked up at Abuelo, 'Is she dead?'

He yelled at me: 'Don't say that!'

I shut my mouth and stared too. He told me to get out of the kitchen.

I stomped back to the bedroom I shared with Abuela and laid down on the bed nearest the door, feeling a lump in my throat, mad that he'd yelled at me. I stared at the ceiling. The room was growing dark. The television was still on in the living-room. I could hear the evening news. I fought back the lump and rolled onto my right side, into the dimness of the darkening sky out the window, and away from the glow of the TV. The television news talked of riots in North Miami. I thought of Abuela and how she looked in the kitchen, pale and waxen. I drifted off.

Josefina returned to Havana in May 1953, with wider hips and a full head of short, wavy black hair. She had been feeling much better. However, by the autumn of that year, Consuelo was not feeling well at all. A hot afternoon in October continued the trend. She was out back hanging washing on the line. She kept having to bend over, take the heavy, wet clothes out of the basket, then reach up as far as her four-foot-ten-inches would take her and place each bit of clothing on the line, securing it in place with a wooden clothes pin. This action she repeated over and over, moving down the line as she went, bending over to push the basket across the grass. Each time she came up, she had a little more sweat on her brow, a little less lift in her legs. Underwear and handkerchiefs, dress shirts and socks waved their farewells to Consuelo from the line above her head. The sun toasted her pretty face and small hands. She could feel the sweat trickling down her spine and pooling in the small of her back. A light breeze cooled the perspiration on her face, a mixed Asian and African face that attracted appreciative looks on her daily walks between the house and the market. It was 3 pm and she just couldn't take it anymore. She had to get some rest.

Dizzy and sleepy, Consuelo turned and headed inside to the relative cool of the Spanish-tiled interior. She came in through the open back door and saw the cook's heavy back-side facing her from the kitchen counter where she stood chopping onions. Consuelo made a quick right into the laundry-room where her cot was kept. She lay down, sink-ing carefully onto the springs so as not to notify the cook, Delaila, of her presence. Consuelo nestled her head into the pillow and sighed in relief as sleep overcame her.

In the adjacent kitchen, Delaila turned from her task and looked out through the kitchen doorway into the sun-drenched back yard. She wiped her thick brown hands on her apron and squinted in order to get a better view outside. She walked over to doorway, probably wincing as usual at the pain in her sixty-five-year-old feet, and stopped on the first step that led down to the patio and out to the yard beyond. She didn't see Consuelo. The laundry basket, how-ever, sat half full under the clothesline.

'Consuelo?' She called in her crackling voice—a voice that had been rich and young when the Cuban constitution had first been adopted. 'Consuelo?' Consuelo heard the first cry, but she didn't want to move. Delaila probably needed something from the market that she couldn't fetch herself. Consuelo could hear her going into the dining-room, steadying herself along walls and chair backs as she went. Consuelo had left the doors to the cabinet that held the Baccarat, porcelain and English silverware open, and a cloth and bowl lay on the table, ready for nimble hands to dust glass and polish silver.

'Where'd she go?' Delaila was probably concerned about all of these things half done. La Dama wasn't in at the moment, but she would be back from an afternoon canasta game soon, and she would see that the house wasn't ready for guests. Consuelo knew this but couldn't budge.

'Consuelo?' Delaila cracked as loudly as she could. No answer. She entered the laundry-room. There, she found Consuelo, eyes closed, nestled into her cot. 'Look at this. Consuelo! Wake up. What are you doing? And today of all days.' Consuelo rolled onto her side. 'Ai, no jodes, Consuelo.'

Consuelo opened her eyes, a thick fog over all she saw. She looked at Delaila for a moment, realizing that she had been caught sleeping in the afternoon. She smiled and pushed herself slowly into a sitting position. She rubbed her face.

'What do you think you're doing? How can you sleep now, leaving the laundry half hung and the dining-room half prepared? How will the clothes dry before you have to take them down so that the guests don't see them? How could you sleep?'

'A little mercy, Delaila. I don't feel well.'

Delaila softened a very little bit, 'What is it?'

'I ... well, lately I'm just exhausted and sometimes a little dizzy—especially in the afternoons. What if I've got something?'

Delaila looked at Consuelo's face, examining every curve, brow hair and angle. 'Tired and dizzy in the afternoons? ... Are your breasts sore?'

Consuelo just looked at Delaila without answering.

Delaila broke her meditation on Consuelo's face. She threw her hands up and shook her head, 'Hijíta, you're pregnant!'

Consuelo bit her lip and shut her eyes, 'What?'

Delaila shut the laundry-room door, 'Pregnant, pregnant. You're pregnant. What have you gone and done to yourself? Who is it? Do you even know?'

Consuelo's mild temper was aroused, 'Of course I know, but it's not important. It's only important that I'm pregnant.'

'When did you last menstruate?'

Consuelo didn't answer.

'When?'

'Over two months ago.'

'Two months? What were you thinking? Didn't you suspect before this?'

Consuelo got up and went to the window where she could look out over the yard and the ceiba tree and hibiscus bushes. 'I just kept hoping that it would start again.'

'Ave María,' Delaila sat her heavy self down on Consuelo's cot. 'Why would it do that, Consuelo? Was this an immaculate conception? If it was then perhaps you've nothing to worry about. Otherwise, you're going to have to do some planning because the Castillos won't have a pregnant maid serving flan to their Yacht Club friends.'

Consuelo remained silent and looked out the back. She tried to enjoy the blooming hibiscus while Delaila ranted on.

'And what about your mother? And your brother? What will they do when they lose the few pesos you throw their way every month? Did you think? Did you think before you did this, Consuelo? Before you took off with some man down an alley? No, I suppose you didn't. Sometimes there is no thinking before these things. No thinking.' Delaila wiped her face with a handkerchief. She brought a small, Spanish fan out of her apron pocket and fanned herself.

Consuelo looked at Delaila, 'What planning can I do? I can clean and wash and if I can't clean and wash, there's nothing I can do, so I'm not sure if that's what you mean by planning, but there—I've planned.' Consuelo started crying and sat on the cot next to Delaila. Delaila took Consuelo's head into her hands and placed it on her breast.

'There, there, niñita.'

'Delaila—you can't tell. Just let me handle it. I need the work—I need to work as long as I can—now more than ever. Just let me work.'

Delaila was silent for a moment. She shook her head, 'Of course. I suppose it's nothing to do with me. I won't say a word. But Consuelo, you have to visit the santera. You have to see what's in store for the baby. And cleanse yourself. Don't leave this to chance.'

Consuelo agreed.

'I completely agree.' Consuelo got up off of the porch step. 'We need more beer. I will go to the store.'

'No, no … I'll go.' I got up and hurried past rabbit and birdcages into the kitchen to stop her from rummaging through her beige vinyl purse for money.

'No, no, I will,' she kept rooting around in her purse and came up with seven crumpled dollar bills.

'No way, I'll go,' the no-no-me-no-not-you-no-me rumba of Cuban politeness was on and it was hard to keep up with Consuelo. I hurried to the living-room door, opened it and stood there for a moment. 'I'll go. I'm quicker. And I have a bike. Be back soon.' I shut the door behind me before she could protest and took off on my bicycle, knowing that the best thing to do in those kinds of situations is to pretend that the culprit is age (you can't go get the beer, you're just not fast enough) instead of money (I'd never in a million years let you buy me a six-pack—you're an old woman living alone in an peeling house raising rabbits and chickens).

The ride down the dirt road was slow. I was going in the

direction opposite to the way I came. It was dark and there were no streetlights. The further down the road I went, the more populated it became. I was bicycling through a silent audience: my way was lit by television and mood lighting glowing from people's living-rooms, and by the lights filtering down from the avenue up ahead. It was a suburban sort of quiet—a quiet that is actually a white noise of television sitcoms, car wheels against asphalt, clicking motors of ceiling fans, the hum of fluorescent lighting in food-marts.

But the gentle noise of Central Florida was a symphony compared to the racket of South Florida. A racket I loved. Traffic five times as heavy; the sounds of disco, salsa, merengue, son and rock emanating from a thousand nightclubs; gangs of muscular young men cruising, hanging out of the windows of their Corvettes, shouting at women who ignored them; the life or death cheering at University of Miami or even little league baseball games; doors flung open, the smell of pork and sound of mad shouting, loud television competing with radio, and raucous laughter at family gatherings—gatherings that every family on the block could hear and participate in from their own living-rooms. I smiled to myself, remembering.

Down where the dirt road met a paved road, I found a small grocery store and parked my bike near its entrance. It was a lone, weathered clapboard structure in the middle of a parking lot paved with buckling asphalt. The plastic sign in the store window said 'Tom's'. Through the window, I could see a chubby Mexican wearing a baseball cap tending the register.

There was a payphone just outside the screen door. I fished a fistful of change out of my jeans' pocket. A few dimes slipped through my fingers and chimed a discordant tune on the sidewalk. After dialing and hearing the amount due from a recording, I pushed enough dimes into the slot to complete a call to Miami.

The phone rang and was picked up quickly by my father.

I tried to sound cheerful, 'Hi.' He didn't answer at first. I could hear his breathing.

'Where are you?'

'In Lakeland. Or near Lakeland anyway. I'm visiting your former maid from Cuba. Isn't that cool?'

'Why would you do that without telling us?' He sounded angry.

'Uh … because I'm interested in family history. I wanted to meet her. Don't you?'

'No. Why would I want to meet the maid? I don't even remember her.'

'Oh, well, but still, she knows our family. She can tell me stories. I can learn more about us. I just wanted … a friend … who knew us. Isn't that great?' I didn't understand why he wasn't as interested as me. Papí is like that. He never stays angry with someone and never thinks over the past, replaying scenes, trying to find their meanings or importance. He just moves on. If a friend hurts him, betrays him in any way, no matter how insignificant, he just writes him off and makes a new friend. I had obviously not gotten the nostalgia gene from him. I held on, clung to, reviewed, tried to interpret everything that ever happened to me.

Cubans are overprotective, and my dad was no exception. 'I'm upset that you went all the way up there and didn't tell us where you were going. We called your apartment and you didn't answer. We were worried about you. Next time tell us. Have a good time with the maid.' He hung up.

I stood there with the phone in my left hand, staring at it for a while. I replaced the handset and leaned against the booth, feeling guilty and annoyed.

Sumido En Su Dolor

I'd cried myself to sleep in the bedroom. I'd dreamed: Miami was going up in flames. Television news stories of the riots must have seeped into my consciousness while I slept. My mother woke me around 8:30 pm. She lifted me out of the bed with a grunt and a heave, and carried me out through the front door and up the outside steps to the apartment on the second floor.

Her trip up the steps was labored. I was getting bigger every day. Mamá took slow steps. Halfway, she gave up and set me on my feet. I trudged up in front of her the rest of the way, squinting when she opened the door to the living-room lights.

Mamá stood in the open doorway behind me. I looked up at her moon-shaped white face and dark curly hair framed by the stars of the night sky and asked, 'What happened? Where's Abuela?'

She didn't answer. I think that she was annoyed by my

asking for Abuela. Mamá resented her role as mother being usurped by the dominant woman downstairs—but Mamá gave in easily to the wishes of older relatives. She was too much of a good girl, had too much of the old Cuba in her and not enough America to fight against tradition.

She led me into the bathroom and told me to wash. I rubbed a wet cloth on my face. Mamá waited for me in the doorway, leaning her strong round figure against the doorframe, looking concerned. She took a deep breath and waited for me to finish. 'Abuela had to go to the hospital.'

I started to cry, 'What's wrong with her?'

She took me into her arms, 'I don't know. She'll be ok, though. She will.' I sniffled against her soft stomach as she patted my head. She brought me into the kitchen and sat me at the table, then turned to heat the carne asada Abuela Josefina had made earlier in the day.

Papí came in then, at about nine o'clock, dirty and tired from a long day at the repair shop. I could see him from my position behind the green kitchen table. He shut the front door behind him, didn't say hello, and went straight for the bathroom. I could hear the door shut and the lock turn.

Papí was tall and lean, with a dark complexion and jet-black hair. He was a lamb but he looked like a lion. He didn't talk much, but when he did, he was all jokes and pleasantries. He had a terrible time taking care of himself, though. Mamá would always be on him to do the simplest things: comb his hair, change his shirt. Papí lived in a universe parallel to Abuela's. Both of them had unique relationships with the day-to-day world. Mechanically gifted, repairing was his main commerce with reality. Both Abuela and Papí were meditative and prone to bouts of lengthy and involved storytelling. Abuela's tales, however, were usually tragedy or romance, drawn from her own life. Papí's were comedies he'd heard or made up. This only made Papí more inscrutable.

I turned to my mother who was at the stove, stirring the beef stew with a wooden spoon, 'Papí's home.'

Mamá didn't pause.

I turned back to the table and looked at the plastic Disney World place-mat and glass of milk in front of me. The place-mat was still a little wet from the wipe-down Mamá had given it. I traced the shape of a car in the water with my index finger and imagined what it was like to drive. I was on I-95 in a Datsun when Mamá put my dinner in front of me.

That night it was difficult to sleep. I tossed and turned and wondered what the hospital was doing with Abuela. Did they have to take her blood or pull her teeth, or give her an injection? Would she have to lay in bed, attached to a machine that made regular beeps, the way patients did on General Hospital? I got out of bed and knelt to pray.

'Dear Jesus, can you help Abuela? I think that she's a saint. I know I'm bad sometimes, but if you help her get better ... I'll become a nun.'

I crawled back into bed feeling better that I'd taken some action.

Consuelo took a bus to visit the santera not long after she realized that she was pregnant. She had great respect for Delaila and always took her advice. If Delaila said that she should go to the santera, then she should go to the santera. Although Consuelo was a believer, she didn't submit herself to meeting with actual santeras or santeros much. She didn't like the blood; in those days, she found it excessive. Of course, what would she know about Chango and what he deemed necessary or not? She tried to do as they prescribed, but it was often difficult and sometimes costly to get the necessary provisions for some of the rituals.

The bus bumped along at a fair pace. As she got farther out from Havana proper, the roads deteriorated. Passengers were picked up at a stop near Guanabacoa and among them she thought she saw the small, round shape of her sister, Lydia. She ducked in panic, hiding her head behind the old man in front of her, but it was a false alarm. Consuelo was on her way to a santera Delaila had been going to for years, someone near Güines, who would not know Consuelo's family or friends and who could not share news of her pregnancy with them.

Consuelo looked out the window. In the oncoming traffic she could see a Ford pick-up truck with peeling blue paint and a load of guajiros in the back. Consuelo imagined that they were headed into Havana to spend their wages on a prostitute or get drunk; but maybe it was just to visit someone. She felt guilty about thinking the worst of them. They probably didn't make enough to have a lot of fun anyway. Why begrudge them a night out?

She started to tear up. She felt bad for assuming the worst about a bunch of peasants in the back of a truck. A lot of things were making her feel teary lately. The other day she was eating a banana and dropped the last bit on the dirt in the back yard. Tears welled up in her eyes as if her dog had been run over in the street. She had felt really stupid and had quickly wiped her tears, picked up the banana and thrown it away. Consuelo wondered if it was the baby making her feel this way, or other things.

She took her eyes off of the road and looked down. Her dress was a light floral print of pink and blue. It was her only nice dress, the one that she used to visit the doctor, go to church, visit santeras and go to birthday parties. Her small, brown hands were folded neatly in her lap, their usual position when she was nervous or waiting anxiously for something. The skin was a bit rough from washing and scrubbing, but her nails were neatly kept and she did her best to rub the lotion she found on Josefina's bureau into them when she could. She just used a dab every now and then—not every day. She used lard or oil at other times. It was that or lose the youthful look and pleasant feel of her hands altogether before she even reached the age of twenty-five. She didn't feel bad about the dab of lotion. Anyway, Josefina wouldn't miss it.

Consuelo was tiny like me. Her feet barely touched the floor of the bus. She was slim and delicately constructed but with an unusual and surprising amount of strength. She had high cheekbones, almond-shaped eyes, rosebud lips and a cute, round nose, a hand-me-down from her mother's side of the family. She looked at the world through the dirty window as if she would never see it again: large mansions with marble staircases, which gave way to rice and cane fields, bohíos, palm trees, a country shop made out of stucco and tin, a man with a donkey carrying a load. She wished that she were in her bed in the laundry-room, sleeping or secretly reading one of Josefina's American *Vogue* magazines.

Within a few hours they arrived in the town of Güines (they could have made it sooner, but the driver insisted on stopping for guarapos and a rest more than once). They pulled up in front of the small Spanish Baroque church in the center of town. Consuelo alighted in the town square with a canvas bag, a piece of paper with an address on it in Delaila's unsteady handwriting, and a gourd filled with water from the Almendares River. She turned to look at the large green bus behind her, disgorging passengers in a steady stream like the river where she'd bent to fill her gourd that afternoon. There was no one on the bus whom she recognized or who could recognize her.

Uneven cobblestones stretched out in concentric circles

from the church into the square surrounded by shops, cafés and restaurants. Well-dressed patrons washed rice and cuttle-fish down with goblets of Spanish wine. Consuelo faced east into the dim street lamps, and breathed deeply the scent of petrol. She started walking, trying to remember the layout of Güines from her memories of having visited her father's family as a child. Her father's mother had died years ago, and since then there had been no reason to visit Güines. The family was all in Havana.

Delaila's directions may have been misspelled, but they got Consuelo to her destination without any problems. At each crossroad that she passed, she placed centavos and hard candy to please Elegua. She had walked for thirty minutes like that, past homes with their smells of dinner, her stomach rumbling, and arrived on the outskirts of town at a small, neatly kept, white stucco and tile house. There was a gardenia bush out front and the sound of chickens and goats coming from the back. Consuelo hesitated before swinging open the white-washed wrought-iron gate. She grew fearful for a moment when she thought she heard the barking of a dog, but then realized that it was coming from the yard of a house down the street. She was rather nervous, though she had been to santeros and santeras before. This time important questions followed her into the yard.

Consuelo put the gourd down at her feet and knocked on the front door with her right hand. She clutched her canvas bag in her left. She waited at the door, staring at the white-washed walls, waiting for her future. A tall, strong woman, pure café con leche wearing red and black, opened the door. She smiled at Consuelo and welcomed her into the house.

Consuelo stepped inside carefully, as if the floor were laid with glass. She clutched her possessions and stared at the santera.

The santera touched Consuelo's hand, 'You're Consuelo? My name is Omara.'

'Yes, Omara, nice to meet you. Delaila told me your name.' Consuelo felt at ease. She looked around at the simple but clean living-room. There was an alter to Elegua behind the door. The couch was upholstered in old red velvet, the coffee table was black wood with gold filigree along the edges.

'I see you've brought what you need.' Omara pointed to Consuelo's gourd and her bag.

'Most of it, I think. Not all. I don't have molasses or toasted corn.'

'I probably have whatever you don't. This way.' Omara started for the kitchen. Consuelo followed in her shadow: Omara towered over her by almost a foot. They walked through the small, dark kitchen and into another room furnished with chairs, an alter with food offerings, candles, a rug in front of the altar, and an empty space on the concrete floor in one corner.

After some small talk, Omara got down to business, 'Let's have the coconut.'

Conseulo pulled a small coconut out of her bag and handed it to Omara who took it in her hands and smoothed it like a baby's head.

'Nice coconut.'

'Thanks.' Consuelo giggled nervously.

Consuelo also took out a red and black candle and put it on the floor where Omara pointed. Omara peeled the outer husk of the coconut, then took it out the back door into the open yard, and stood on a small concrete patio. Consuelo saw her tall moon-lit form lift the coconut and smash it on the patio. Coconut milk splattered across the cement. Consuelo shivered. Omara called Consuelo out to the patio.

'Pick four clean pieces, not little chips. These will be your obinús.'

Consuelo studied the coconut pieces by moonlight. She wanted to pick just the right ones. Which would give her the answer she longed for? She touched several lightly with the tips of her fingers before picking four large chunks. Omara brought the gourd to the doorway.

'You got this water today, yes?'

'Yes. It's my day off. I walked to the river and back with the water.'

Omara took the coconut pieces from Consuelo and rinsed them in the river water. The pieces went in and out of the water like children at a baptism. Consuelo wished them well.

After they were rinsed, Omara stepped back into the darkness of the room with the pieces of coconut obinú in her left hand. With her right hand she picked out three bits of coconut meat from each obinú.

Omara chanted, 'Obinú ikú obinú ano obinú eyo obinú ofó arikú babagwá.'

Consuelo felt a thump in her chest.

Omara put the pieces down on the floor and lit the candle to Elegua. She placed the candle in front of his image and the pinches of coconut meat on a plate next to the candle. She took a gourd filled with Saraceo mixture and added some witch hazel, which Consuelo handed to her. She poured in some of Consuelo's Almendares River water and made a thin paste. She placed the gourd with the paste next to the coconut pieces and the candle as an offering to Elegua. Omara took the bottle of river water up again and sprinkled water around the offering, while chanting, 'Omi tutu ana tutu tutu laroya tutu ilé.'

Consuelo watched Omara perform the ritual, heart pounding with worry and anticipation. Omara then picked up the gourd with the thin paste and spilled a little in each corner of the room. She threw a few drops out of the door.

Omara smiled at Consuelo, 'It's an offering for a favorable reading. Now, let's pray to Elegua. If you don't know Lucumi you can pray in Spanish. Remember, these are like yes or no answers, so the request should be fairly simple, or the divination will fail. Or Elegua could mislead you.' Consuelo nodded. Omara commenced the prayer, 'Elegua laroye akiloye aguro tente onú apagurá akama sesé areletuse abamula omubatá okoloofofó okoloñiñi toni kan ofó omoró ogun oyopna alayiki agó.'

Consuelo knew enough to pray along with Omara in Lucumi, but when Omara was done Consuelo closed her eyes and composed a little prayer of her own. 'Elegua, please,' her voice broke. She gathered herself together to continue, '... please let me be able to provide for this child. Please let it be healthy.'

Omara went on to pay respect to other orishas, chanting for each. She led Consuelo in honoring the spirits of her dead. A vision of her father's mother flashed in her head, followed by her father, a short, strong, and happy man. Consuelo asked permission in absentia to throw the biague of her godmother, Delaila, the one who had been present at Consuelo's initiation into the religion. Consuelo bent down to moisten her fingers in the spilled river water.

Finally, the moment had come. Omara took the coconut obinús and touched them to Consuelo's forehead. Consuelo closed her eyes and inhaled deeply. Omara threw them on the floor like dice.

Consuelo and Omara stared at the pieces for several moments. One obinú was white meat side up. The other three were dark shell side up. Omara didn't look pleased. Consuelo didn't know how to read the oracle, and she searched Omara's face, trying to decipher the answer. She held her tongue, waiting for Omara to speak. She waited for a while, as Omara examined the shells without touching them. When she could wait no more, she spoke, 'Well?'

Omara looked up at Consuelo from her crouching position, examining the shells. 'He says ... no.'

'No? What do you mean, no? What does he mean?'

Omara stood up, her frame towering over Consuelo. 'Well, what did you ask?'

'To be able to take care of my child. For the child to be healthy.'

Omara looked back to the shells. 'We could try it again. See if he still agrees with his first assessment.'

'Yes, please.'

Omara performed the ritual two more times, but the outcome was the same. 'I won't try this again, Consuelo, we may really anger Elegua this way. He'll get bored. Come outside, we'll do a cleansing.'

Consuelo was devastated. Omara took her hand. 'My dear, the obinús are telling me that you'll lose the child. But ... keep faith, perhaps Elegua heard your questions incorrectly.'

After the aborted conversation with my father, I peddled quickly back to Consuelo's with the six-pack, burning off some of the annoyance I felt at being reprimanded at this age. When I got inside, I saw that Consuelo had laid out a spread for us. The beans she'd been simmering all afternoon were now in a serving pot in the middle of the table. In addition to these there was white rice and sweet fried plantains, as well as some leftover roast pork from the day before that she had reheated. The beers had made me hungry and I was grateful for the food—it was delicious. Abuela Josefina's cooking was very good, but Consuelo's was superb. Cubans are black-bean connoisseurs, and Consuelo's beans were definitely superior—their consistency a creamy blackness, the beans melted in your mouth, the ingredients in harmony. We ate in silence for a while, Consuelo's TV on so she could see the late news. The stories dealt with a drugs bust and a murder in the Orlando area.

After dinner we had cafésitos. Consuelo smoked, and obviously decided that she'd talked enough for one day. 'Marysol, I want to know abou' you, my dear. You are very quiet, jus' listening to me. You're young, but I bet you have stories, too.'

"What kind of stories?"

'You know, family stories. How is you father?'

'He's fine, thanks. Working hard as usual.' I didn't know what else to say about my dad.

'And your Mamá? I have never meet her. Her name is Luz, right?'

'Yes, that's right. She's fine, thanks. Same thing—long days as a seamstress, but she always finds time for me and Papí. In the evenings, she likes to make me pretty dresses that I never wear, because I have nowhere to go in them,' I laughed.

'How did you parents meet?' Consuelo smiled.

'Oh, they've told me this story a million times …'

Juan thought, 'This is a rotten way to spend your fourteenth birthday.' He stood with Josefina and Rogelio in the waiting-room. They held on to each other by arms, shoulders and hips. They each carried only one suitcase and had no one to see them off on their last day in Cuba. Josefina and Rogelio's parents were long dead, and Ricardo and Barbara were already in Miami. Josefina's other brother, Oscar, had joined the Revolution.

The airport was a scene of controlled chaos. All around Juan, Cuban families played out the same refugee drama: tears, hugs, exhortations to behave and listen to the aunt in New Jersey, the grandfather in Orlando, the priest in Miami. Grandparents hugged children. People talked of big plans when they arrived in Miami, big plans. Men stared out the windows at the tarmac, the airplanes, the outskirts of Havana in the distance, with the hollow look of the starved. Emotions were equal parts desperation and hope.

Juan was shaken to the core by these displays of emotion, heightened even by Cuban standards. He didn't understand leaving. It hadn't sunk in. He was sure that this would be just like going to the indoctrination schools in the countryside—something from which he would return. And Josefina and Rogelio were convinced that they'd one day return to a Castro-free Cuba to reclaim what was rightfully theirs. Juan, however, didn't think that the Revolution was going to collapse in on itself any time soon, but he couldn't imagine that he would be leaving it all behind forever, either. It seemed like next week, maybe, he would be back at school in Havana, Josefina back to standing and waiting several hours a week for meat rations, Rogelio back to the docks driving a truck—an assignment from the Revolution. Dad has told me that the human mind can't grasp that kind of change in one go, and if it could, the heart wouldn't believe it.

Then, into the waiting-room came familiar faces, as alone as the Castillos: the Diaz family. Josefina and Rogelio hadn't seen them since late 1957. Mercedes and Roberto Diaz had moved with their daughter to Pinar del Río in the late fifties to run a tobacco plantation, but the Revolution had turned their plans upside-down. He had met these people as a little child, but he couldn't remember anything about them. Juan could see from their faces that Mercedes and Roberto

48

were as desperate to leave Cuba as his own parents.

Josefina smiled, overcome by the pleasure at seeing friends in the same predicament as she was and going to the same place. She nearly shouted, 'Mercedes!' Mercedes smiled widely and waved. The Diaz' seemed thrilled to see someone they knew as well. They joined Rogelio, Josefina and Juan, and began to chat about the past, about who was in Havana, who was in Miami, and what they were all doing to earn a living. Juan was bored by their conversation, but not by the look of their teenage daughter, Luz.

Juan had looked at girls with some interest before, but looking at Luz was like looking at a woman for the first time. She was tall and strong, had pale skin and dark hair, a round shape … she looked older than her fourteen years. She was, as far as Juan could tell, the best looking girl he'd ever seen.

'Consuelo,' I laughed a little, 'Mom's good looking, it's true, but it needs to be said that he went to an all boys' school, and spent summers laboring in the countryside with other teenage boys, so I don't think he'd really seen that many women. I think he's probably glorifying his first sight of her somewhat—typical Cuban man.'

'So, he's a romantic.'

'Exactly …'

Juan was not as physically mature as Luz. I can tell this myself from photographs of them at that age. But he did have one thing on his side: height. He was taller than most boys his age, having started his growth spurt early. Luz was about six months older than Juan, and tall, but they could face each other eye to eye. Nevertheless, Juan couldn't pluck up the courage to actually look her in the eye at any time that

49

afternoon. He stood during their time waiting to be processed sneaking looks at her, and her at him. They didn't actually say anything to each other apart from the obligatory hello and kiss on the cheek when they first met. Then they boarded the plane, sat in different parts of the cabin, and didn't meet again until a week later in Miami.

When the Castillos arrived in Miami, the government assisted them into temporary accommodations near Coral Way. The Castillos reconnected with the Diaz' while standing in a line for government food the following week, and they clung to each other. Josefina and Rogelio had the support network of Ricardo and Barbara, and the Diaz' had some cousins in West Miami. By combining their web of contacts, the Castillo and Diaz families helped each other into work, and into a new, Cuban-hued America.

Juan and Luz were enrolled into the same co-educational public school. Now, Juan could lay eyes on as many girls as he wanted, of all different shapes, colors and sizes … but he kept eyes only for Luz. He is a safe man. He likes known quantities, measurable amounts and distances. He doesn't go in for the unknown and he didn't in this instance either.

In 1969 Juan initiated the Cuban courtship ritual and started going round to the Diaz household to see Luz almost every evening. If he arrived early enough, he would be treated to dinner. They were not actually allowed to go on a date, even with a chaperone, so they would sit together on the front porch of the Diaz duplex, the window wide open so Roberto could keep an eye and ear out for the pair while he read the newspaper in the living-room, his easy chair strategically placed so that he could see them, but they could only see the very edge of him.

Juan estimates that they spent hundreds of nights on that porch, counting the terracotta tiles on the floor, watching the moths buzz around the bare light bulb that hung overhead, Juan's feet resting on the metal railing that separated them from the small front lawn and the quiet street beyond, him telling funny stories he'd made up. They would close their eyes to feel the breeze on their faces, looking out at a suburban Miami that had all the elements of their homeland—the same plants, grass, people, temperature, colors—but that looked like a tamed, controlled, dulcet-toned version of Cuba, hemmed in at the edges by chain link and a functioning democracy.

'They married young, like so many of my friends' parents, after Mom turned eighteen in December of 1971. By the end of 1972 they'd had me.' I smiled, 'Isn't that a nice story?'

'Yes it is. Thank you, Marysol.' Consuelo looked tired and dreamy, 'Let's go to sleep, is very late. Tomorrow we can go to the Waffle House for breakfast.'

Consuelo and I woke up around eight the next morning. We had Cuban coffee and cigarettes in the kitchen, and then fired up her old pick-up truck to head for waffles down on Route 98. It was funny to watch her drive. She sat really close to the steering wheel and peered over the dashboard at the road, the lights and the oncoming traffic. We pulled into the parking lot of the Waffle House in stops and starts, and she finally managed to ease us into a parking spot.

Inside, we got a table by the window and immediately ordered coffees. Around us were truckers on their way down to Miami or up to Gainesville or Atlanta. They sat at the counter or at booths, tucking into large plates of pancakes, waffles, eggs and bacon, occasionally shifting their bellies in order to get more comfortable. There were also mothers with children, and a small Girl Scout troupe was in the back, eating their breakfast in a very orderly fashion.

Consuelo and I ordered waffles.

'So, you said when you were nine, Josefina got sick again and had to go to the hospital? Did she lose her hair again? I hope not, it was so beautiful.'

I sipped from my mug and thought with pain and a little shame about that period. The pain I could understand, but I wasn't sure where the fiery hot shame burning in my chest and cheeks was coming from. I was uncomfortable talking about that period. I never talked about it. I never wanted anyone to know that my Abuela had been in a mental hospital. But if I couldn't talk about it to Consuelo, there would never be anyone I could really share it with.

The waffles arrived and I asked the waitress for more coffee.

'She didn't lose her hair again, no. She'd gone, I suppose you could say, catatonic about mid-week, maybe a Wednesday ...'

On Saturday my parents and I went to the hospital to see Abuela. The hospital was beige and quiet. We ascended in the elevator, surrounded by other visitors who were also beige and quiet. When we reached Abuela's floor, we got off and walked down the hallway to the left, heading for a big set of double doors. The doors were locked and there was a buzzer and intercom to one side. Mamá pressed the button. After a moment two large nurses, identical in their monumental whiteness, opened the doors for us.

Once inside, I was surprised to see that most patients were not in their beds looking like death, with drips hanging from their arms and attached to machines repeatedly sounding, 'Beep ... Beep ... Beep ...' but that they were walking around in their hospital gowns and robes, smiling and talking.

They all looked pretty healthy, I thought. We passed down a hallway and into a large visiting-room. Here, there were more patients wandering around in their robes and playing checkers and watching television with their guests. The atmosphere, however, was strange. I got this sense of sus-pended animation. The patients seemed to be running in place. There was tension among their visitors. Some patients smiled and waved at us when we entered. I smiled back.

We found Abuela Josefina in a wheelchair, sitting by a large window, staring out at a panoramic view. You could see Miami stretching out, low white buildings in the brilliant sunlight, a patchwork quilt spread to the horizon where it met the Everglades. Glowing pastel and neon civilization bordered by sea and sharks on one side, alligators and swamp on the other. There were arteries of traffic cutting through the neon quilt, station wagons and sedans rolling purpose-fully towards mysterious destinations in a never-ending flow.

Josefina was in the same state that she had been since Abuelo Rogelio found her. She didn't notice our approach or our arrival. I touched Abuela lightly on the hand. 'Abuela?'

There was no response. Mamá took my hand and led me to a seat along the wall. Abuelo was sitting in a chair next to Abuela, smoking a cigarette and whispering with my father who had to practically bend his tall body in half to hear what Abuelo had to say.

Mamá patted my hair. I looked up at her soft, milky face. 'What's wrong with her? Is it a fever?'

Mamá looked up at the television on the wall, showing *Three's Company*. 'Kind of. There's a fever in her mind, and she can't act like she usually does because she's sick.' Mamá looked down at me. 'You know when you have a stomach ache or a cold, you don't act the way you usually do. You have to lie in bed, stay home from school, sleep, you don't want to play … I mean … this is the same thing. She just can't talk to us right now.'

'Ok, I understand.'

Mamá looked pleased. Abuelo Rogelio, however, looked terrible—like he hadn't slept in days. I'd been staying upstairs all the time with Mamá and Papí since Abuela went into the hospital. In the afternoons after school, when Mamá was still at her shop working as a seamstress, I stayed with one of the neighbors: either Marielena and her granddaughter Gladice or Gabriella and her granddaughter Maria. I couldn't stay with Mamá's parents because they had passed away when I was smaller, one right after the other. In the evenings, Mamá and I would go downstairs, bringing Abuelo his dinner, and watch a little television with him. Eventually we'd have to go to bed, but he would stay in front of the television with his glass of scotch and water, quietly sipping the night away.

Papí pulled a seat up beside Rogelio and sat down next to him. Mamá and I watched TV next to Abuela Josefina, pointing out funny bits in the show and trying to engage her in our world. At one point, Mamá went over to Abuela's wheelchair, took a comb out of her purse and tried to comb her hair the way she knew she liked it. But this was difficult because a stylist usually did it, and Mamá was no stylist. She did her best, and then kissed Abuela on the cheek. Abuela stared out of the window, unmoved by the gesture.

I was happy to see Abuela wasn't dead. That night earlier in the week, when Abuelo Rogelio had found her at the kitchen table, staring out the window like a zombie, I thought her lack of movement was due to something much worse than a fever. Now I supposed that she probably just needed a rest from the housework and me shouting and running around the house.

Mamá came back and sat next to me. She put the comb away in her brown leather purse, sighed once, and looked back up to the television set. Papí came over to us, sat down beside me, and smiled. I looked up at him. I thought he was so handsome with his dark eyes and cappuccino-colored skin. His straight black hair was slicked back. He was very tall and slim, quite unlike Rogelio, who was stronger, with stocky muscles, probably from all the work on the docks.

'Papí, are you sad?'

'A little. Are you?'

'Yes. I want her to come home. I'm not happy she's here with all these strangers.' My voice descended to a whisper, 'They're a little weird ... and Gabriella across the street never has any cookies or chocolate. She's always giving me fruit after school! I definitely want Abuela back.'

My mother interjected, 'Juan, tell her she should be eating more fruit and less candy.'

My father smiled, and pulled me up onto his lap. 'A little fruit won't hurt you, mi niña. Be sure to be grateful to the neighbors, they're very nice to take you in. You get to play all afternoon with your friends, and—'

'Marielena makes me do homework first!'

Papí laughed, 'That's good. Discipline ...'

We were silent for the rest of the visit, not speaking to each other, not looking at Abuelo Rogelio who occasionally gave out a big, miserable sigh. We just sat and stared at the TV or out the window, like Abuela Josefina.

'She improved quickly after that, thankfully. She wasn't in the hospital for too long. She lived to tell me more tales. She just needed a rest, you know.'

We were back in the pick-up now. Consuelo had insisted on showing me the sights of Central Florida. I issued a condition that none of these sights could include amusement parks or wacky muscums, and she was hard-pressed to come up with anything else for me to see. We drove around for a while, looking at some of her favorite farmland; at an unpaved, dusty trailer park she used to live in; at her Southern Baptist church located in a strip mall next to a McDonald's; and the local Salvation Army shop where she liked to get her clothes.

We stopped at a red light. Consuelo was silent for a moment, waiting patiently for the light to change. She didn't seem very satisfied with my explanation. 'A lot of us need rest, but some of us never get a rest. We work our fingers to the bone. There is no rest for us. Why does she need a rest?' She huffed.

I was taken aback. This was the first time Consuelo had shown any negative feelings towards Josefina.

Y Arriesguemos

Within two weeks, during the early morning hours, Fidel and his bunch would take Moncada, or try to. That day would be Josefina's twenty-sixth birthday. Josefina and Rogelio planned to have the household in Santa Clara by then, in preparation for the late mango harvest. Some years they went together, some years only Rogelio went. This year, the whole household would remove to the countryside. Josefina saw it as an escape from the sameness of the city.

The dance would be their last party before retreating. The 26th of July Movement would start without fanfare; Josefina, however, was most celebrated in her Christian Dior. She circulated among attendees, smiling widely: straight, perfect teeth glinting in the lights. Her hair was thick and curled, her diamonds heavy on her fingers and ears, but she bore this without complaint. She was approached by a man she had known since her childhood in Oriente. Rubén Castro smiled and said hello. She smiled, too, asking how his brother was faring, 'Still a radical?'

Rubén looked slightly uncomfortable, 'I imagine so.' But he didn't want to talk about Fidel, he wanted to talk about her. About her small dog and her last trip to Spain, about shopping in New York and what she was reading. Little did she know at that time that he was to be attacking the military barracks at the other end of the island in just a few days. Rubén flashed a smile and leaned against the bar.

She thought, 'He's grown into himself.' Rubén was a few years younger than her. His smile had been perfected; he'd grown a bit of a mustache, giving definition to his youthful face. His eyes were large and round. He didn't have his brother's extreme good looks, his intense extroverted charisma, but Rubén made up for it in personal charm— warm gazes that excited her, the ability to seem honest and caring and extremely interested in what she had to say. He was muscular, young, intelligent and full of possibilities. His appeal to her was completely different from Rogelio's. Rogelio was older, staid, conservative, cool. He was intelligent, but it was a slow, measured intelligence that didn't allow you to glimpse its machinations. With Rubén, you could see the neurons firing behind his eyes; connections being made that had not been made before.

'But he was a wayward communist, too attached to his bourgeois habits. The homeless in the parks and the starving guajiros in Camagüey or Pinar del Río were more his brother's concern. He wanted to support a cause he thought was cutting edge. He felt that there was no use clinging to the past. He thought Fidel was the future, he could sense it. Rubén was not one to be left behind.' Josefina took a sip of her iced tea, looking meaningfully over the rim of her drinking glass at the other women.

We were out in front of the house in the late afternoon, slouching in pastel-colored plastic lawn chairs. Abuela Josefina's trouser legs were rolled up, an unusual move for her, testimony to the sheer heat of the day. I was in the chair next to her licking an ice-cream cone. It was 26 July, the anniversary of the raid on Moncada, the true inception of the Revolution ... and Abuela Josefina's birthday. She was sixty-one. I was fifteen. Abuelo Rogelio had told me he would bring home a butter-cream cake, some flowers and a Chinese takeaway. I was to ensure Josefina was not down gossiping with the neighbors when he was due home so that he could surprise her.

Abuela had finished her long day of chores and I'd finished a long summer's day of doing nothing at all. I'd wandered down to my cousins' house earlier to see if they were in, but no one was home. I'd then gone in the other direction up to Coral Way, to see if there was anything of interest on at the movie theatre. Nothing appealed, so I picked up an ice-cream cone at Carvel's, and walked the three quiet blocks home in the stinking heat, dragging myself the last few hundred yards, fearing heat exhaustion all the way. And there was Abuela Josefina, in a lawn chair, shading herself under short palms, surrounded by the Old Cuban Lady Nostalgia Club, all of them fanning themselves in unison with painted Spanish fans, sweat beading on their temples. Josefina had saved a seat especially for me. I'd sat down, mint chocolate-chip ice cream streaming down my cone and sticking to my fingers. I'd licked it and leaned back, relaxing myself, settling in for a nice chat.

Josefina tried to cool herself down with her fan. She addressed her audience, 'I was his type, you know ...'

… slim and long, green-eyed with a shock of thick black hair framing her sharp features. Her tongue was a blade that could cut, but Rubén told her that he was sure she made up for it in bed.

Josefina placed her champagne glass down on the bar. Rubén immediately called for another from a waiter passing by with a tray. He carefully lifted a glass off of the engraved silver and held it out to Josefina with a smile.

'For you, beautiful.'

Josefina smiled coquettishly. She took the drink out of his hand and took a sip. 'I love champagne.' Her eyes drifted away, surveying the guests.

Rubén scanned the crowd, too, looking for Rogelio, patting his neck with a handkerchief as he looked. He spotted Rogelio in the dimly lit ballroom, whiskey in hand and big, sad eyes on a full-figured fake blonde. Rubén smiled and looked at Josefina.

Josefina had spotted Rogelio, too. Her eyes narrowed as she sipped champagne and scrutinized him. The blonde stood dangerously close to Rogelio, against a wall near the band. They were partially hidden by a flower arrangement, but nothing could ever seriously impede Josefina's precision radar.

Rubén saw Josefina seeing Rogelio. Josefina caught him looking.

The band started playing a cha-cha-chá.

Rubén held his arm out to Josefina.

She grabbed it before he could even ask, and followed him through tables of women in shining gowns, around mulattos holding trays, to the polished dance floor in front of the band Las Congas de Felix. They cha-cha-chád vigorously.

She looked at the room from different angles: up to the

60

crystal and gold chandeliers; over to the long, polished wood bar; around at the guests and the fountain in the center of the room, spurting pink water in thin rivulets. And she saw Rogelio. She saw him as he took the arm of the buxom faux blonde and walked her to a table in the shadows, then leaned close to hear her every word.

The cha-cha-chá ended. The band started a salsa romantica. Lovers flooded the dance floor, surrounding Rubén and Josefina, making them a small, still island.

Josefina pulled away from Rubén and pushed her way off the dance floor. Rubén tried following, but despite her three-inch-spiked leather pumps, she was quick. She took a glass of champagne from a tray and went into the ladies' room.

Josefina stared at herself in the mirror. She focused on the fine lines making tracks below her eyes, furrowing deeper every month. She traced one of these with her finger, following it slowly from where it started near her tear duct out to where it submerged itself in her soft, peachy cheek. She looked over and noticed a small black woman in the corner holding towels. Josefina had not realized that there was anyone in the room with her. They stared at each other for a moment. She took a lipstick out and dabbed pink on her lips. She fished out 25 centavos and tossed it on a metal plate in front of the bathroom attendant. The woman neither smiled nor frowned, nor made any move to pick up the change. Josefina turned to go.

She stood by the open bathroom door, peeking around the corner at Rubén, waiting for a moment when his attention was distracted. He was drinking a highball at a table near the ladies' room, waiting patiently for her return. She quickly slipped out of the ballroom, tapping out across the marble floor and downstairs. She crossed a large Persian rug in the reception area, her heels leaving small pockmarks in the surface. She wanted some air. She'd told me and others about this walk many times: every year on or around the 26th, she remembered.

From the Malecon, the bay that opened into the Florida Straits could look fierce. On stormy days the spray reached many feet above the sea wall. It shot up like a great ghostly hand from the water and splashed down on passing cars. If you were walking along the sidewalk that bordered it, you could get drenched. But on calm nights, it was the best place to stroll. Havana twinkled beside you like a melon pierced with gold. The clubs along the water were lively. The big-band sounds mixed with the ocean to form a poly-rhythm composed of wave and conga, which carried the passerby along the waterfront on a cushion of beat.

Josefina wanted to take a walk along the Malecon. She wanted to walk alone, take a break from Abuelo. She couldn't stand him chatting to Lourdes. But instead of eyeing him fiercely, or making a snide comment, as would normally be her way, she just left the ballroom with a glass of champagne in hand. When he found her missing, Rogelio would be worried. Maybe he would be angry. She smiled to herself, relishing the thought of him hopping mad at her for a change.

Josefina knew she looked lovely in her gray dress. It accentuated the green in her eyes and made her look positively feline. She was sipping champagne, walking quickly, proudly. Before long, she sensed Rubén following not far behind. He must have seen her slip out and had followed, but not too closely. She later found out that in his pocket were directions to hand out to Havana-based supporters for the early morning: on the steps of the University of Havana, they were to shout, they were to yell, they were to proclaim the Revolution. They were to wake the neighborhood and convince every passerby that Batista's regime was soon to be over.

Josefina was not many steps ahead of Rubén now. She turned to see him empty his glass in one draft and throw it over the sea wall and into the bay. She picked up her pace, her desire for him having slackened when she saw Rogelio with Lourdes.

Josefina was frightened when she heard steps running up behind her. She swung around suddenly, raising her glass above her head, a reflex action.

Rubén stopped near her, 'Did I frighten you?'

'Of course, you fool. Why are you running up behind people in the dark?'

'Why are you out here all alone? You're dripping with diamonds. Aren't you a little worried?'

Josefina leaned against the sea wall petulantly, 'It wasn't foremost in my mind. I needed some air.' She looked around her. 'Besides, there's plenty of activity around here. There's all those men standing in front of that jazz club over there.' She pointed across the avenue to El Cotton Club.

Rubén looked in their direction. 'I wouldn't trust those fools. What could be on their minds, eh?'

Josefina didn't like the tone of the conversation. She took a close look at Rubén and realized that he was thoroughly smashed. His eyes were wide and glassy.

'Very well. Perhaps you're right. I'll go back to the hotel.'

'Why go back so soon? You're with me now. I'll look out for you. Where would you like to go?'

Josefina bit her lip. She looked around her, lamenting the decision to leave the dance. 'I'd like to go to the Hotel Presidente ballroom.'

Rubén tried again, 'But Rogelio is at the hotel.'

'So what?' She spat this out. She had lost patience with him. He acted like a fool sometimes, easily swayed by that self-absorbed, bullying brother of his. Sometimes her impatience got the better of her and she let it show. She softened her tone, 'He's my husband. I don't mind seeing him.'

'Why did you leave?'

'I told you, I just needed some air.' She lost her cool, 'Why are you pestering me, Rubén? What's your game? What do you want?'

Rubén reached out and grabbed Josefina's skirt. He couldn't reach her thighs for all the layers of tulle. She reacted with a yelp and slapped his hand with hers.

'Let go. You're drunk—let me go.'

He pulled her towards him and put an arm around her waist. She put one hand on his chest, and in the other, held the champagne glass above her head threateningly.

'Rubén, leave me alone. I've known you since you were a little thing in diapers following your brother around like he was Jesus Christ—don't do this. Think of Rogelio. He wouldn't be pleased.'

'You undermine your own intentions. I just want a little kiss,' Rubén puckered his lips and strengthened his grip around her middle.

Josefina was annoyed, 'Lord, don't make me yell, please.'

'No need for yelling. Why not a little kiss? That's all I want. You're so lovely.' He leaned in towards her. She struggled against him.

'Rubén, this is it. Back off, or I'll disfigure you.'

Rubén didn't back off. Her arm descended, champagne glass intent on damage—or at least scaring him a little bit. He caught her wrist.

'You wouldn't hurt me, would you?'

She had a moment of panic and she thought of Santiago de Cuba. The panic subsided as she raised her leg and put her Italian leather heel down firmly on Rubén's toe. His eyes seemed fit to burst from their sockets. He released her, and grabbed his foot with a gasping inhalation. She brought the champagne glass down on the back of his head. It shattered. He yelled. Blood flowed down his neck, staining his white collar.

Josefina turned and walked briskly across the avenue to El Cotton Club. The doorman admitted her without question. She walked through the tables crammed with tourists and prostitutes, past the potted palms to the bar in the back, where she ordered a martini.

'Rubén went to the hospital that night, not out to drum up support for the attack. The next week, after the raid on Moncada, Fidel was jailed with the others. Rubén fled to Mexico. No one leafleted the neighborhood surrounding the University of Havana. The Revolution was postponed, but not cancelled.'

I looked at Josefina. I had to squint, as the sun was setting behind her head. I was starting to get skeptical about her stories. I didn't think she was lying, exactly, I just thought: can all of it be true? Can someone's life be filled with that much drama? I looked around at my surroundings: the kids playing in the street in their white sandals and shorts; the chubby Costa Rican woman on the corner pruning her lime tree with oversized shears; an El Dorado passing slowly down the street, taking care to avoid the children; the Cuban ladies, overweight, tired looking, sipping iced tea. It all seemed so serene. It was hard to imagine a revolution, a hundred miles away, and people like Fidel Castro's brother loving Abuela Josefina. What if most of her stories were fiction? Did it matter?

'He really loved me, you know.'

'Fidel's brother loved you?' My tone was skeptical.

'You don't believe me?'

'No, it's not that, it's just, why would he love you? I thought you, everybody, hated the Castros.'

Gabriella chimed in, 'We do.'

Abuela sighed, exasperated, 'I shouldn't have to justify myself to a little flea like you.' Flea was often used as an endearing term, but in this context it had an undercurrent of deprecation. 'But there was a time, before the Revolution, when we thought they would perhaps sort things out. We'd had many changes in government, coups, but we didn't really know what revolution meant. We loved. If you don't believe, then ask somebody else!'

'Abuela, I was just asking … I just wanted to be sure I understood, that's all.'

But I did investigate her story a bit further.

I knocked on the door to 3425 S.W. 26th Street. Rosa opened the door. Her hair was messed up. She looked sleepy and squinted at the midday sunshine coming into her front yard.

'Hey watcha' doing?' I smiled and walked in, brushing past her and into the house. Their fierce-looking but mild-mannered Doberman Pinscher, Pablo, bounded up and nuzzled my hand. He was very eager, and his legs splayed all over the Spanish-tile floors, trying to get a grip on the slippery surface.

'Pablíto, sweetie …' I scratched his ears.

'You're up awful early.' Rosa closed the door.

'It's two o'clock.'

'Right, as I said.' She dragged herself into the small, green galley kitchen, rubbing her face and I followed behind. She got some Coke out of the fridge, lit a cigarette, and drank straight out of the two-liter bottle.

'Rough night?'

She took another swig. 'You have no idea.'

'Sara still sleeping?'

'I think I heard her get in the shower ... she'll be out soon.' She held the bottle out to me and I took a drink.

Sara and Rosa were my cousins. Sara was older than Rosa by about eleven months. They were only a few years older than me, but in my view they were much wiser in years. I idolized them and made it a point to stop by as often as possible to see if I could elbow in on their fun and get their make-up leftovers, boy tips, and stories of their wild nights out. If they found me a nuisance, they never said it, though I must have driven them crazy.

Their house was a few blocks from ours. They lived there with Abuela Josefina's brother and sister-in-law, Oscar and Isabella. Oscar was a graphic designer, and somewhat temperamental. Supposedly, he felt 'betrayed by the Revolution'. Isabella worked at the Lancôme counter in Burdines, downtown, and was as sweet as dulce de leche. I always felt she was chasing after Sara and Rosa, trying to get them to settle down, not stay out so late ... but Sara and Rosa were more wild and rebellious as a team than they would have ever been on their own, and never heeded Isabella. Sara had dropped out of high school at sixteen and Rosa followed suit when she was the same age. They were now busy having bags of fun and trying to figure out what to do with their spare time. I envied them terribly.

Sara wandered into the kitchen, her wet hair tied up into a towel turban, and wearing a short, silk robe. 'Hey sweetie.' She gave me a kiss on the cheek, 'How are you?'

'Fine, thanks. Just thought I'd stop by for a chat.'

'I'm next for the shower!' Rosa left the kitchen. I heard the bathroom door close down the hall. Sara found the Coke bottle on the counter and poured herself a glass. She lit a Winston.

'We're going to the mall ... want to come?'

We pulled up to Dadeland in Sara's brown Camaro. It had roach feathers hanging from the rearview mirror, and a tape deck. I loved the car, even though I had to scrunch myself in the back, and it was hard to hear what they were saying in the front seat because of the Stevie Nicks they played at full volume—the speakers were behind my head.

We found a parking spot towards the back, shaded by a tree. Sara turned down the music and Rosa pulled out a joint. Rosa lit it, each of the girls up front took a drag, and passed it back to me. I took hold of the joint and stared at it, not smoking. I passed it back up to the front.

'So have you found your future husband yet?' Rosa asked just before dragging.

I felt myself blush, but fortunately, they couldn't see me. 'What do you mean future husband … don't know about future husband … but I am dating.'

'¿Qué?' They both shouted in unison.

'You actually have a boyfriend? Hallelujah, 'cause I thought that would never happen,' Sara laughed.

'What do you mean … I'm only fifteen …'

'I was on number three by then,' Rosa added.

I rolled my eyes. In my opinion there was no comparison between Rosa and I. She was tall and had dyed her hair blonde. She was very slim and very shapely, and very, very outgoing. I was shorter, of average build and was a bit shyer about talking to boys. Rosa was bright and happy, and I could be a bit dreary sometimes. Sara had a more curvaceous figure, and again she was vivacious, talkative and bright. 'Of course you'd had loads of boyfriends by my age. You actually spent your time doing something other than homework, and may I mention you're both gorgeous? Anyway, most of the guys in school are gag-me-with-a-spoon gross.'

'So you are not dating someone from your school?' Rosa asked.

'No ... listen, I'm not actually dating anybody. I sometimes study in the library with this guy from my pre-calc class, but he has a girlfriend ... it's, like, all in my mind.'

'You are such a goody-two-shoes Cuban girl, I know you, you'll end up very well, and very safe. You'll marry a decent, church-going, pest-control man or insurance salesman, and you'll have two or three kids, and you'll raise them well, and you'll be happy.'

'I am not safe ... I'd say you're wrong there, I'm not safe ...' I bristled at this. But they were totally right; I was safe. I imagined myself a rebel of some sort, despite perfect school and church attendance. I never made waves.

Sara and Rosa passed the joint between them. Sara held the smoke in her lungs, and let it out in a long, slow exhale, 'Are we going shopping or what?'

We got out of the car and headed towards the mall. The heat undulated on the parking lot, a giant, concrete mirage. I couldn't wait to reach the front doors and have the icy cold air-conditioning raise goose bumps on my arms.

Once inside, we wandered around window-shopping, everyone too mellow to care or want to try on any clothes. We got drinks from Orange Julius and sat down on a bench to watch people walk by with their shopping: teenagers in large, loud, laughing gangs, their upper arms poking out of sleeveless T-shirts; couples holding hands, their pants hiked up above their midriffs and securely fastened by belts, or their bellies hanging over, white sneakers on their feet; South American kids with curly black hair running with ice-cream cones. The mall: the central focus of South Florida fun. It was a microcosm of the community and, I thought, a desperate, boring way to spend an afternoon. I was there weekly.

The pot started to wear off a little after a while, the girls becoming more talkative, and I was able to pursue the line of questioning I had in mind. 'You guys, you were born in Cuba.'

'Yeah, but we don't remember a thing … we came over when we were really young, just kids.' Sara said.

'Yeah, well, have Oscar or Isabella ever talked about the Castros?'

They chimed in unison, 'Constantly.'

'And … have they ever talked about Josefina and Rogelio, and their relationship?' At this, Sara and Rosa looked at each other. That was all the answer I needed—they had obviously gossiped about this many times in that household. 'I can see that answer is yes. Anyway, I just want to know, have you heard about the night of the Revolution … well, some night around the time of Moncada? Josefina's party.'

'From a million different points of view.' Rosa slurped up the last of her orange juice.

'Did Rubén Castro love Abuela Josefina?'

Again, Rosa and Sara looked at each other, but this time I didn't know what it meant.

The woodland-green and campus-cream Chevrolet pulled up in front of the house in the Vedado, loud engine in a quiet night, the dawn not too far away. Josefina sat in the back of the car, staring out the window. Kiki Hernandez turned around in the front seat to smile at Josefina. Her mink stole obscured the big grin she was dishing out.

'You sure you don't want to come home with us?'

Joey joined in from the driver's side, 'Josefina, really, come with us.'

Josefina looked at Kiki. She could feel waves of pity emanating from the front seat. Kiki was doing a good job of

70

hiding it, but not a perfect job. Josefina bristled.

'No thank you.'

'Josef—'

'No thank you. You're very kind, thank you, but I won't. Thanks for the lift.' She quickly got out of the car, before they cooked her entirely with their pity. She shut the door to the behemoth vehicle as quietly as she could out of respect for her neighbors and her own sleeping staff. She let herself into the gate at the bottom of the drive, turning to wave Joey and Kiki Hernandez off with a quick twist of her wrist and flutter of her fingers. The car drove off slowly.

Chichi, old now, waddled up to her and licked her ankle. Josefina lifted the faithful old bitch, cuddling her. She opened the door and brought Chichi into the house. She tossed her fox stole on a chair and kicked off her heels. She sat on the faux Louis XV and rubbed her feet. Chichi wandered over and sniffed her toes.

'The Malecon is not kind to women in Italian shoes, is it Chichi?' Chichi stared at her. Josefina scratched the dog's head and ears. 'You are lovely and faithful my dear, but you are really no substitute for a husband, a child or a lover.' Chichi continued to stare. Josefina smiled at the dog and leaned back in the chair to look out of the window.

She listened to Havana at night.

I looked over at Consuelo, examining her face, illuminated by the fluorescent lights in the discount store on South Florida Avenue in Lakeland. We were picking up a few things she needed: bird food, rabbit food, cat food, sponges, a small waxen statue of Lazarus, a Christ candle, some plastic rollers for her hair.

'She had woke me when she open the door. Chichi had a collar that jangled. I heard the little dog in the house, where she usually was not. Rogelio didn't like animals in the house … well, he didn't like them in general, really.' She put her items on the counter to pay. A teenager chewing gum and wearing thick black eyeliner and neon-green lipstick rang them up on the register.

I rolled my eyes. 'No wonder I could never get a dog! I begged and begged and begged at birthdays and Christmas … but no luck.'

'Well, he thought they were dirty.'

Consuelo was awakened, probably first by the front door opening and closing, but definitively by the jangle of the dog's collar. She lay in bed for a while rolling from one side to another in order to try and drift off again. She heard talking … she lay there, maybe for an hour. Finally, she decided warm milk was the only hope. She got up off the cot in the laundry-room, ensuring her yellow cotton robe was buttoned around her. She found her sandals and, opening the door as quietly as possible, she flapped out to the kitchen. She lit a candle, lit the stove and put a small pot of milk on a low fire.

She could smell the smoke of Josefina's cigarette. It was curling in under the door, enticing her. Out the window in the kitchen Consuelo could see the clothesline and the tops of the trees just discernable in the rising sun. She sighed, looking at the milk. There was nearly no point now, she thought, she'd have to be up in an hour or so. She patted her stomach. She should probably go ahead and drink it anyway: a little extra ration for a little extra reason.

Consuelo heard the sound of the Castillo's Ford pull up in the driveway. She quickly turned the fire down to hush the sound of the bubbling milk. She poured it into a glass, put it on a plate, and blew out the candle. She glided over to the doorway and blew on her milk to cool it off. She took a sip. It singed her lip. She blew on it a bit more.

She could hear the front door open and close. No voices, but heavy steps—Rogelio's. The plock of Josefina's cigarette box opening and dropping shut after a cigarette was extracted. A match was lit. Consuelo pushed lightly at the swinging door to the kitchen, glad that she'd recently oiled the hinges. She slipped into the dining-room, holding firmly onto the milk glass, inhaling its sickly sweet fumes, and peeped through the dining-room door, left ajar by Delaila. Across the hall and through the archway she had a silhouette static blue vision of the Castillos.

Rogelio was standing a few feet from Josefina, watching her smoke. He reached over and lit a side lamp. A golden haze filled the room. Chichi was on Josefina's lap, enjoying a pat.

Josefina stretched, pointed and curled her left foot, folded over her right leg.

Rogelio took a cigar from a humidor on a shelf along the wall. He clipped the end with the cutter in his pocket and discarded it in the same ashtray into which Josefina tapped her Partaga. She stared at the cigar end as it bounced in the crystal. Rogelio puffed on his cigar. Neither spoke. Their competing smokes and scents battled for supremacy in the room, the cigarette smoke—thinner—rising higher than that of the cigar.

Consuelo sipped on her milk, enjoying the unexpected entertainment. Putting the glass back on the plate, it made a very, very slight tink.

Rogelio looked up in the direction of the dining-room door. He and Conseulo stared at each other. Consuelo froze. They stared at each other for a good five seconds, she thought. There was no question, he saw her. And he said nothing. His gaze returned to Josefina. Consuelo withdrew, away from the crack in the door, back against the china cabinet very gently lest the Lladro tinkle in response to her movements.

'I felt like I had broke into The Big Secret. I was no in the marriage, but I seen the core kernel of it in front of me. It had become a threesome,' Consuelo interjected.

We were in the car again, Consuelo's purchases at my feet in the cab of the pick-up. We'd stopped at the lakeshore and were sipping Cokes from Burger King cups.

'Did you slink back to your room then to give them a bit of privacy?'

Consuelo sipped on her Coke, and didn't look up at me.

'She saw us,' Abuela Josefina paused. She was washing clothes in the back yard, the stick going up and down, round and round in the metal tub. 'I wasn't too happy about that.' My Abuela was getting a little too old for this kind of rigorous washing. Rogelio had bought her a washing machine a few years ago, but for the tough stains he picked up working on the docks, she still liked to soak and pound them by hand.

'Will you let me please have a turn with the stick?' I tried to grab it away from her, but she wouldn't let me.

'No, you'll ruin your hands.'

'Abuela ... give me the stick! Let me help you!' At fifteen I was finally starting to get a little bit taller, and a little bit stronger ... but years of washing had made Abuela stronger, and she wouldn't let me help her.

'I tell you no! The last thing I want is for you to learn how to wash clothes. You just sit down there now with your book.' I had brought my science textbook out to the steps on the back yard to try and get a little sun while I studied. It was biology and I was trying to come to grips with the finer points of mitosis. However, it was foolish trying to read quietly around Abuela, who loved to talk as much as I loved to listen.

'Right, so then what? So what if the maid saw you and Rogelio talking?'

'You read your book.'

'I'm done with the homework on this chapter,' I lied.

Abuela believed. 'Well, it matters because what happens, what's said between a man and a woman in their marriage, is private.'

I smiled a bit at this comment because I, and every woman on the block, knew the details of their marriage and everything said in our household from one week to the next. We knew everything happening in everyone else's house, too.

Maria's grandmother, Gabriella, had sent her husband, sick with a bad liver due to thirty years of daily Black & Whites taken neat, to sleep in a single bed in the extra room when she discovered his thirty-seventh infidelity. The first thirty-six didn't seem to bother her much, but somehow the number thirty-seven had some sort of magical quality to it that made her go on the offensive. Gabriella was over-spicing his food and undercooking his chicken. Mario, knowing what was good for him, ate his food without complaint— eyes watering at the sheer volume of chilies in his stew and throat gagging on the bloody pink flesh inside his chicken legs.

Gladice's grandmother, Marielena, meanwhile, had stopped speaking to her daughter Marta, when Marta had contravened some specific advice as to what to do with Gladice, her own daughter. At age fifteen, Gladice was busy sleeping with any boy who smiled at her. The Guzmans were mad with exasperation. They didn't know what to do with her. Gladice went to private school, was in the chorus at the

Presbyterian church down the road, they had the most money on the block—but none of this could help to keep Gladice from being bedded by boys from every part of town.

I suppressed my smile, 'Oh, I see, yes, privacy. Well … surely you can tell me … why did Abuelo Rogelio come home late?'

'He was just staring at me, puffing on his cigar, saying nothing …'

Josefina chose to break the silence, 'So, you've come home.'

Rogelio puffed on his Romeo Y Julietta once, twice. 'Well, I live here.'

A beat. Neither spoke. Hiding in the dining-room, Consuelo finished her glass of milk.

'But you sleep elsewhere.'

Rogelio smiled, 'You've always a comment. A retort.'

Josefina smiled, then frowned.

'Anyway, I don't know what you're so angry about. I lost sight of you altogether. One minute you were talking to Rubén, the next minute the both of you were missing … where did you go?'

'I needed air.'

Josefina suspected that he may actually have been jealous for the first time in years. His brow furrowed, 'Air with Rubén? I presume it was hot air. Where'd you go with him?'

Josefina thought for a moment about telling Rogelio the truth, but almost instantly did away with this notion. 'Enough of this shit—I saw you with Lourdes. My god, a blonde nonetheless. If you're going to go for a fake, at least make it a redhead. There's a bit of interest to them, more style.'

'We were talking.'

'Baa! Yes, talking. I hear she's a brilliant conversationalist, can tell you the ins and outs of "in and out" anytime. I'm assuming you didn't discuss Tolstoy.' The pats on Chichi's head were getting rougher and rougher, so the dog hopped off Josefina's lap. She lay on the other end of the settee. Rogelio leant against the window ledge.

'I left her after you walked out. Anyway, she was talking to me.'

'Two size 36Ds were talking to you.'

'Ai, Josefina, you're getting vulgar.'

Josefina stood. 'Don't give me your "Ai Josefina".'

'I'm telling you I was looking for you!' Rogelio was raising his voice. Josefina shushed him. He started pacing the room, followed by a trail of cigar smoke.

Josefina stopped smoking for the first time in hours. 'You didn't look very hard, did you, because I've been here since 3:30!' Rogelio's only response was to puff on his cigar, roll it between his fingers, and wipe his brow with his Irish lace handkerchief. 'And you've been looking for me where?'

Rogelio turned to face the large portrait of Josefina, on the wall over the French Provincial piano. 'Kiki and Joey helped me. We drove around in the Chevy for hours looking for you.'

Josefina smiled. She felt satisfied. She lifted Chichi, cradled her in her arms, and left the room through the hall that led to the bedrooms at the other end of the house, leaving Rogelio to finish his cigar.

De Gobernantes Indeseables

The first letter came late in the year. It took over a month to make it from a village in Mexico to Havana. It was delivered in the early morning, with the American clothing catalogs, and a postcard from Josefina's brother, Oscar, who had fled to Mexico after the raid on Moncada.

Josefina was just in from a bit of exercise, riding her bicycle up and down the street. She was wearing slacks similar to ones she had seen on Katherine Hepburn in a magazine. She bounded up the steps, in an unusually good mood. She was a bit warm and looking forward to a cooling bath. She met the postman on the front steps. He gave her an unusual look as he handed her the bundle of letters, smiled and walked away, off to complete his morning rounds.

Josefina stepped inside, and started flipping through the mail in the hall. She was happy that her catalog had arrived. She was slightly annoyed that Oscar had had to flee to Mexico, so she put his postcard into her back pocket to read later. Then, she saw it: a letter addressed to her, with a Mexican postmark, and a ringed brown stain, perhaps coffee, in the lower left corner.

She ripped the letter open and read it there, standing in front of the gilt-edged mirror in the hallway, light proffered by the small window placed high above the front door.

She immediately felt bad about the night on the Malecon. Rubén was being aggressive, but she'd felt like she'd overreacted with her old friend, probably out of anger at Rogelio. She knew he'd been drunk, but it hadn't been her first run-in with a drunk man.

Rubén apologized for his behavior on the seawall the previous July, and expressed his deep desire for her. He begged for her forgiveness and claimed to have been intoxicated by the 'drink, the night, the breezes off the water, you.'

Her heart beat a little faster, despite herself. She leant back against the marble of the tabletop in the hall, holding the letter in her hands, looking at each fold's crease and studying the handwriting. She'd never gotten a letter of the sort from any other lover. Rogelio could hardly be called a romantic. And Juan—a boy in Santa Clara she'd met during autumn breaks with her family visiting the farm—was sweet, but not the letter-writing sort.

Rubén Castro, however, was sexy, educated, interesting. Everyone knew he and Fidel were the sons of their father's cook, but the cook's children dominated the house and were treated like equals. They'd been sent to boarding school, university, and given a stipend for living—money Rubén mostly spent on drink and women.

She shook herself out of her reverie. This man had tried to take advantage of her. He was a rebel. He was in jail!

She looked back at the letter. He seemed sincere.

She folded the letter, left the rest of the day's mail on the hall table, and strode into the house to bathe and change before drafting a reply. After her bath, Josefina put a cloth around her head to hold her hair back and smeared a thick layer of cold cream on her face. She wrapped herself in her pink terry robe and sat at the bureau to write.

They wrote to each other regularly after that, their letters a *pas de deux* of seduction. Josefina was simultaneously aggressive and coy. She consistently pushed him away, which only encouraged his passion. The crueler she was in her letters, the gentler and more loving he became in his. Her strategy was to back him into uncomfortable emotional corners, again and again, force him to apologize, force him to profess his love—again and again. She loosened up, slowly. She paced her disbursals of mercy and affection to him, lest he pull away too quickly, move on to more challenging promontories. She slowly reeled him in, Rubén seemingly unaware of the emotional quicksand he had stepped into, the line on which he'd been hooked. The mail came in the daytime, when Rogelio was not around, and she could keep her entertaining and exciting secret to herself.

I sat staring at the diaphanous paper, amazed at the words. 'They are so passionate, Abuela, they take my breath away!' We were in the bedroom I shared with Abuela Josefina. Abuelo Rogelio slept alone in the other room.

Abuela smiled at me, 'Me, too. When I need to have my breath taken away, I take the box down from the shelf. I try not to do it too often, so it doesn't lose its punch.' Abuela Josefina took the shoebox from me, carefully took the paper back, and folded it into the box. She put the top on the box and held it securely on her lap, as you would a baby.

'I can't believe you kept them all—all your letters, all your memories, all the way from Cuba. I can't imagine receiving letters like that.'

Josefina sat down on the bed beside me, 'Things aren't the same anymore. You have cheap telephone rates now. Nobody writes letters. The mail just brings bills, legal documents, maybe a Christmas card. But also, men were different back then. Cuban boys now are nice but they've grown up under Fidel. I don't think you'll find men like the ones I used to know anymore.'

Though I would have loved to receive a passionate letter from one of the better-looking boys in high school, I was thankful that they didn't make them like Rogelio and Rubén anymore. 'That's not a bad thing. Abuela, these guys had control issues. And I don't think they knew much about women.'

'Control issues?' She looked at me blankly.

'I mean … they have to control everything. There is no room for chance, for free will—your will. They can't handle anything that deviates from their plans. They want you to do what they want.'

'I know that about them. But I share these stories with you to show you that no matter what, even when others in your life try and control you, there are ways for you to be free.'

It had been a long, hot day. Consuelo and I had had fun traipsing around running her errands. We were back at her house now, on the sofa in the living-room, the windows and French doors at the back open so the lake breezes could cool us down, the ceiling fan whirling rapidly to speed the process. I kicked off my combat boots and wiggled my toes.

It was so wonderful to meet someone who I'd only held in

my imagination for so long. We were having a giant puzzle-making session, using personal history as our pieces, trying to fit them together, ensuring that there were no gaps, ensuring that we weren't forcing misshaped memories in with each other.

I looked over at Consuelo, who was holding a Cuban coffee in one hand and a cigarette in the other. She was not looking directly at me, and seemed a little dejected.

'What's wrong, Consuelo?'

She didn't answer immediately. 'I'm surprise they wrote letters to each other.'

'Really, why? The letters seemed so romantic.' Consuelo flinched. She stubbed out her cigarette.

'I just don' see what those two had in common. I mean, he was one of the "architects of the Revolution", and she … was so bourgeois! Her main concerns were movie magazines and hairspray!'

I somehow felt that this was an attack on me. 'I don't think that's fair, Consuelo. You know that's not true. Josefina had other concerns … she read books, she wasn't totally out of touch.'

Consuelo looked grumpy, 'I'll give her that.'

'I'm not sure where this is coming from.' I looked searchingly into Consuelo's face, trying to read her motives, and to understand what undercurrent of emotion I'd tapped into.

We were quiet for a while. Consuelo finished her coffee, not looking at me. The late afternoon sun slanted on the lake. It looked like a still photo. It was quiet out there on that summer, weekday afternoon. There were no boaters, no children, no neighbors wading in the water or fishing. People were inside, preparing dinner, or resting after a long day at play. Finally, Consuelo broke the silence.

'Come with me.' She pushed herself off of the couch

lithely in spite of her sixty-year-old body that had spent a lifetime cleaning, bent over buckets and floors or stretching to reach laundry lines. I followed her down the hallway off the living-room, the old black and white tiles cool under my bare feet. There were simple rooms in this part of the house, decorated mainly with plain bed sheets and crucifixes on the walls. She led me into her bedroom at the back.

'Have a seat on the bed, if you like.'

I did. Consuelo pulled a small drawer open in her dresser. It was filled with correspondence. She pulled out a packet of letters tied with a graying shoelace. She sat down beside me, untied the shoelace and laid the letters down between us on the bed, spread like a fan.

They were old letters. I instantly recognized the postmark, and the handwriting, 'Rubén Castro.'

Consuelo smiled at me. 'I learned to read and write only a little as a child—my brother taught me enough to read the headlines on the newspaper, read and sign my name. But I learn how to read and spell the big words I used in the letters to Rubén for two reasons: Josefina taught me writing in the afternoon when she was bored, and I practiced reading her magazines. You are right, I was no fair to Josefina just now.'

I stared at Consuelo. I was shocked. I ignored any other points she may have been making and seized on this one: Rubén had been writing to two women in the same household—never mind betraying the Revolution!

'Were you jealous?'

'What do you mean? I didn't know until you told me today!' My heart squeezed tightly. I felt terrible guilt. My big mouth … all the stories … I'd hurt her. I teared up.

'What! Why do you cry? What is this? No, stop,' Consuelo went out to the bathroom to get me some toilet paper. 'Here, use this. Don't be ridiculous. This is more than forty years ago. There is nothing to cry about anymore. I have done all of my crying, enough for the two of us. Now stop that.' Consuelo put her arm around me. 'You are a grown woman now. You know about these things. Men are not …' she searched for the right word, but it eluded her, 'perfect, I suppose.'

I tried to calm down. I wasn't making anything better by crying. I was only crying because I felt bad for myself—that I'd done something wrong. I tried to smile at Consuelo.

'You're right, there's no reason to cry.'

'Listen, don' worry, I had my secrets from Josefina, too.'

The room was dim, lit only by a bare light-bulb in a tall, thin wooden floor lamp. The smell of workingmen's shirts at the end of a long day mingled with that of expensive cologne, the kind Rogelio wore. In the air were accents of the more common violet water used in most Cuban households. These scents were punctuated by the intoxicating and slightly nauseating smell of ink, seeping up through the floorboards from the printing presses below. There was not much room to move. Consuelo had arrived late, and she was pressed up against the back wall, unable to see a thing. She stood on her tiptoes while clutching at her cloth bag, straining to see the man speaking at the front. She couldn't.

The tall man to her right smiled down at her and said, 'Let me help you.' He put his arm around her small shoulders, and with her safely under his muscular wing, he pushed them through the crowd, excusing himself politely along the way, until the two of them were near the front, and Consuelo could see the speaker. He was a short, sweaty man with a mustache.

Consuelo smiled up at the man who had helped her, 'Thank you, Señor González.'

'Miguel.'

'Miguel.' Miguel looked back to the speaker, and Consuelo, as discreetly as possible, made a mental daguerreotype of his features: long, strong Spanish nose; large brown eyes; light brown skin; wavy hair down below his ears, brushed back, held in place and made shiny with pomade; thick lips, which concealed a perfect set of small white teeth. Consuelo looked back to the speaker, Armando.

'... And that's why the fight must be fought. We shouldn't allow this island to be run by American gangsters. We shouldn't allow this island to be driven into the ground by the immoral apes with which Batista socializes. Trust me,' the speaker pounded his chest, then raised a single finger in admonition, 'Trust me, they mean you no good. For every dollar that comes into this island, they will take 75 cents. There will be nothing left for you, there will be nothing left for your children. Under this system, under this yoke, our future is slavery, prostitution, endless toil in the sugar-cane fields so American companies profit ... crime, drugs— there's no respect in this system. Don't fool yourselves—no respect. Don't let the American tip his hat at you, and say thank you, and flash his teeth and don't think, even for one second, that you can be his equal, because comrades, you cannot. You will never be. The relationship must change.'

'¡Asi mismo!' People in the room called out and clapped, including Miguel. Consuelo stood clutching her bag, smiling vaguely at the speaker, wondering if he knew Rubén personally.

Miguel González had come by her mother's house several days ago asking for her, inviting her to a meeting. Consuelo had been at work at the time, but on her day off she went looking for him in a local café, as per the message he had left, in order to see what business he had with her. She found him

85

sitting at a table in the rear. His back was to the wall, and he was facing the window. The rusty paint behind him was peeling. Miguel González sipped a coláda. Consuelo nearly fell backwards when she saw him. She thought he was the finest specimen of a man she'd ever seen. It was only at the meeting, however, that she really got a good look at him. On that first encounter in the café, it had been like looking into the sun—she couldn't stare for long.

Miguel was a member of the 26th of July Movement. He had learned about Consuelo's existence through the grapevine, a grapevine that started at the top, and he had invited her to a 'meeting'. She was told she should not tell her employers about this meeting, or indeed even co-workers, unless she thought that there were some particularly disgruntled with the government these days.

Consuelo had told no one about the meeting. She was interested in what was going on, and excited to be included in something that sounded so important, but in addition, deep down inside her, she felt that attending the meeting was a way of getting closer to Rubén.

When the meeting ended, everyone started chatting with each other. Miguel was speaking with Armando. Consuelo didn't know anybody. She stood around shifting from foot to foot, smiling at nobody and nothing until, after not too long, she left.

A Hallar Sin Tregua

I climbed the few tile steps up to the entrance of the ground-floor apartment of our house. Inside, Josefina was in the kitchen, cooking. The smell of picadillo filled the house, laying a thin film of garlic, tomato and olive oil on everything. Josefina called out from the kitchen, 'Oh, there you are!' She seemed surprised that I was home.

'Yes, here I am.' I walked through the small living-room and into the kitchen. Abuela was standing near the bubbling pot, smoking a cigarette. A *Vanidades* magazine was opened on the table.

'Did you have a good afternoon?' She took a drag, eyeing me sharply.

'Yes. It was ok. I visited Sara and Rosa. We just watched TV. Nothing much. I can't wait for school to start again in August—I'm actually starting to get a little bored, and sick of the library.'

'Mmmm.' She took another drag, not taking her eyes off of me. I started feeling uncomfortable.

Staring right back at her, I asked, 'What?' curtly. As I got older my ability to tolerate Josefina's passive-aggressive moments was waning.

'You know … you have to be careful.'

I rolled my eyes. Oh dear, lecture on the way, and I couldn't figure out for what.

'Don't roll your eyes at me, sit down! I tell you if we were in Cuba, it would be five lashes for you out by the ceiba tree.'

Sighing, and trying not to roll my eyes again, I sat at the end of the table, in her usual chair. I looked at Abuela Josefina. Her eyes were on fire. They had a distant look—she was recalling moments of the past.

'You've been spending afternoons with a man … in bed.'

'No!' I was truly shocked by this allegation. Where was she getting this from? 'No I'm not, what are you talking about? … I've been spending afternoons at the library or with Sara and Rosa—just finding something to do out of the heat that doesn't involve the shopping mall!'

'Marysol, don't lie to me. I know these things, I know them.' She stabbed her cigarette out. She was going into her paranoid psychotic mode. I'd seen this state before, usually aimed at Rogelio. I couldn't believe I was at the receiving end. She was often on target, but this time she was way off.

'Ok, I'm … why are you thinking this of me? Where would you get this stuff?'

She softened her tone. 'Marysol, you're getting older now, and there are things you should know.'

I panicked. 'No, no, Abuela … I don't need the sex talk. I'm sixteen—gonna be seventeen. I know about sex, we don't need to review that, I understand about sex.' I really wanted to head this conversation off at the pass, get it off the table, strike it from the agenda.

'You know about sex … you know about sex, yes, the mechanics. But there's more to it than chromosomes and ovulation. There's love, and there are babies.'

I steadied myself. My fingers pressed against the plastic on the tabletop, the tips turning pink and white from the pressure. There was no way out of this lecture.

'You know how babies are made?'

'Yes, all about it, Abuela. Sperm plus egg equals baby. See? I know, no need—'

'You have to watch how much time you spend with boys.'

I bristled, 'Boys! I wish. I haven't even been out on a date yet. I only see boys for school projects and studying and as friends. And it doesn't matter how much time I spend with boys, does it? It's what we spend it doing, isn't it?'

'One thing leads to another. You think you're in control, and then it's gone. You may not even realize that you're being seduced—but you are.'

'Abuela—'

'Quiet and listen.'

Consuelo came in from the back garden with a load of dried washing. It smelled warm, of the sun and gardenias. She put it in the laundry-room and went out to the dining-room, where she could sit in a comfortable, straight-backed chair.

She had the same sick taste in her mouth. It wouldn't go no matter what she tried—galletas, bits of bread, avocado pulp, mango slices, mint leaves, sugar-cane juice—nothing could take the taste of sick from her mouth. It was permanent. It was taking her appetite away. In general, the tired feeling was starting to wane and she was gaining energy, but that particular symptom had been replaced by the sick taste.

She rubbed her face with her hand.

Josefina was out at the shops. She wouldn't be home for lunch, as she was meeting the women of the Cuban-American Friendship Club. They said that they did fundraising activities, but to Consuelo their gatherings seemed excuses to play canasta for hours on end. When Josefina came home, in any case, she never came home with plans to build a new hospital or a rural school, but details of her wins and losses.

The front door opened and closed. Consuelo quickly stood up from her seat, grabbed a rag from her apron pocket and held it at the ready, as she thought it could be Josefina coming home. But it was Delaila who opened the dining-room door and entered carrying a net bag with sour oranges, garlic and cumin. She would use these to marinate pork and yuca for the evening meal. Out of sympathy for Consuelo's state, Delaila had taken to running some errands for herself.

Delaila removed her straw hat, untied her scarf, and wiped the sweat from her forehead. She put the groceries down heavily on the tiled floor and smiled at Consuelo. 'How are you today? We haven't had a chance to chat at all. You've been out there pounding and hanging the whites all morning.' Delaila eased herself into a chair next to Consuelo.

Consuelo smiled at Delaila, who was more of a mother to her than her own mother—a woman with so many preoccupations that she had barely attended to Consuelo as a child. She'd been considered well able to fend for herself. 'I'm better. Not as tired as before, but now I've got this taste in my mouth—it won't go away.'

'It'll go away, but you have to wait a little while. The sick taste is a good sign. You'll have a healthy baby.'

Consuelo was stung by this comment, 'Not according to the santera you sent me to.' Consuelo stopped and stared at Delaila, who stared back.

'But you said the visit had been "fine" ... Well, don't just stare at me, what did she say?'

'Elegua foretold the loss of the child.'

'Oh, no. I better make a pot of coffee.' Delaila took her supplies into the kitchen. She was in there for a little while, during which time Consuelo sat quietly, staring at her small hands with their small fingers. She wiggled them, astounded at the amount of washing they had seen, and hoping they would one day hold a baby. She hadn't rubbed oil into her fingernails for a while, and she noticed that they were short and cracked. It would be best if she didn't have long fingernails for the baby. Anyway, long fingernails would get in the way when she was dealing with the clothes, or lifting things. They would never grow, what with the tasks she had in front of her. She sighed. She thought of Josefina's long fingernails with envy. 'Well, what do you expect? She doesn't have to get them sullied.' Consuelo was surprised to find that she had said this aloud, to no one. She smiled at herself, feeling embarrassed.

Delaila returned with two tiny cups of coffee on a small tray. She put the tray down on the table and then sat next to Consuelo. They reached for their coffees in silence. The coffee had already had plenty of sugar stirred into it by Delaila in the kitchen. It tasted hot, strong, and sweet.

'Thank you, Delaila.'

'No hay porqué ... So, Consuelo, tell me.'

'Yes?' Consuelo was reluctant to tell the santera story, as if repeating it would make it come true, like repeating a prayer or a curse.

'Tell me ... tell me exactly what the santera said. Tell me exactly what Elegua said.'

Consuelo sighed. 'Well, it wasn't good. The biague landed with only one coconut flesh visible, face up. The other three were shell side up.' Consuelo sipped at the small coffee cup, wanting to prolong her rest period, and savored the sugar dregs at the bottom of the cup.

Delaila thought on this news for a moment, eyes rolled up to the sky as she ran through a history of interpretations in her own head, finding a positive spin for the gloomy prediction. 'Well, my dear, it could have been worse.'

Consuelo squinted her eyes at Delaila, 'How could it be worse?'

Delaila finished her coffee in one sip, knocking her head back and afterwards licking her lips with gusto. She smiled. 'You could've gotten all four shell sides up—Oyekun. That's most certainly death. There's no way back from that prediction, you know. There are possibilities with what the santera told you. Maybe Elegua didn't hear you properly.'

'That's what she said.'

'Maybe he's playing a joke on you. Perhaps you've not been praying enough to your orishas? Not sacrificing, showing them your respect?' Delaila gave Consuelo a chastising, schoolmistress look.

'I can't afford the sacrifices! Goats, chickens, it would ruin me.'

'In any case, don't lose hope, don't give up on your baby. Never give up, Consuelo.'

'How did you manage it when your children were babies and you had to work?'

'For the first child, a girl, we were desperately poor. I couldn't work. My husband, God rest his soul, cut sugar cane down Güines way. We lived in a hut, but I kept it clean. We lived the same way for the second child, and the third. Manuel died shortly after the fourth child, Octavio, our only son, was born. I simply had to come to Havana to work. I took the girls out of school and we came to the city. The oldest girl got odd jobs running errands, washing and such. The middle girl watched the children. The third girl, about six or so, was the only girl to go to school. Octavio, he also went to school. That's because I've had this job with the Castillos for a long time and they've been very good to me.'

'They can be taskmasters.' Consuelo looked at the mountain of silver in the case on the table, which she had to polish before the day was out, in addition to laundry, serving the Castillos, dusting …

'But you have a job and you should do it well. They're kind otherwise. They let me sleep in my own apartment with my children. They helped me to send Octavio to school. He can read and write, and knows science.' Delaila smiled with pride, 'And now Octavio works for the electrical company. He doesn't make much money yet, but he will.'

Consuelo thought about Delaila's words. Things had certainly seemed difficult enough for Delaila, but despite their rural, peasant lifestyle there had been one distinct difference between Delaila's situation and Consuelo's: Delaila had had a husband when the first child was born. By the time he'd passed on, Delaila could count on support from the older girls to help. Consuelo had no one. There was no one in her mother's household, no low wage-earner such as a twelve-year-old girl, who could stay home from work or school to look after the child, not even her mother. Consuelo would have to go home, squeeze into the room with the four of them and beg for what she could get from her mother's earnings.

'Thank you, Delaila. There's no way out of it now: I'm pregnant, the baby's due in the spring, and I'll have to make it work, one way or another. Everybody does it, I suppose, and that's just all there is to it.' Consuelo smiled at Delaila, who frowned and focused her eyes behind Consuelo's head at the doorway to the sitting-room. Consuelo turned.

Josefina leaned against the doorframe, staring at her

unsmilingly. 'Can you get me a cold drink, please? Bring it to my dressing-room.' Josefina closed the door behind her. Consuelo could hear her heels tapping on the tiles, their tiny echoes disappeared into the cool afternoon atmosphere of the house. Silently, she and Delaila went into the kitchen.

Consuelo squeezed lemons into a pitcher, added cool water and ice cubes from the Frigidaire, and stirred in large quantities of sugar. She poured the lemonade into a tall Baccarat—choosing Josefina's favorite drinking glass to placate her. She placed it on a tray with a napkin and two crackers centrally positioned on pink porcelain. She wiped away any crumbs. She put a gardenia she'd picked from the back garden in one corner. Delaila stared at Consuelo, but Consuelo looked away and, lifting the tray, pushed through the swinging door and out of the kitchen.

Walking through the sitting-room, she looked out through the window and saw peace and quiet in the front garden, not even a bird, no one at the gate, no one on the sidewalk or in the street. The afternoon was lazy and quiet. Women, children, husbands were in for siestas. Or perhaps they were not at home at all. The car of the Machado's across the street was not in the carport. Perhaps Armando was at his club, or at his import-export business, or parked around the corner so he could sneak into the back bedroom with their maid, Margarita, his lover.

Consuelo concentrated on her tray in order not to spill anything. She walked into areas of light and dark cast by shut doors, open doors and curtains, the skylight several meters down the hallway—an American affectation that made a terrible noise during the rainy season. She stepped carefully into Josefina's bedroom. The door to the adjoining dressing-room was closed, so she carefully balanced the tray on one arm, and knocked with the other.

'Come in.'

Consuelo opened the door. Josefina was sitting at her vanity table, staring at the open racks of clothes in front of her. Josefina's shoes were kept safely in boxes, or lined up in neat rows underneath her skirts. Consuelo knew them all. She washed, treated, pressed and polished anything that wasn't strictly required to be dry-cleaned by professionals. She knew the labels—the same labels she read about in Josefina's *Vogue* magazines. She knew the small rents in fabric and places in seams that were particularly vulnerable to separation, especially after long dinner parties or nights of dancing.

Consuelo placed the small tray in front of Josefina at her vanity table, carefully pushing aside Max Factor powders, pancake make-up and lipsticks. She backed away from the table and stood politely in the middle of the dressing-room with her hands folded behind her back, waiting to be dismissed.

Josefina looked at the tray. 'I didn't ask for crackers.'

'I thought you might be—'

'I didn't ask for them.'

Consuelo didn't reply. Josefina didn't dismiss her. Consuelo's breathing became shallow. She could feel her heart pounding against her sore breasts.

Josefina took a sip of the lemonade. 'It's nice.'

Consuelo tried to smile, but was only able to curl one side of her mouth, the other quivering.

Josefina sipped again, 'I like your lemonade.'

'I know. I thought I'd make you lemonade instead of—'

'Yes, ok.' Josefina, brows furrowed, waved a hand at Consuelo to cut her off. Consuelo, assuming she'd been dismissed, turned to leave. 'You're going? I'm not done.' Consuelo turned back to face Josefina, slowly. Josefina was staring at Consuelo's face, studying it, but Conseulo refused to meet her gaze.

'You're pregnant?'

Consuelo let out a long exhale. Josefina had heard her and Delaila in the dining-room. Consuelo had held false hope for several minutes, but now there was no doubt. 'Yes.'

'Hmmm.' Josefina drank her lemonade again. She fingered the cracker, but decided against it, letting it drop back onto the porcelain. It cracked and crumbs spread onto the tray. 'That's not good. You're not married. It'll be hard for you to care for the child on your own.'

Consuelo didn't look up.

'Who's the father?'

Consuelo didn't answer. She tried to show no expression on her face. She thought about the chores awaiting her that afternoon: take in the whites, iron, serve dinner for the Diaz' who were coming for a casual dinner …

'Consuelo, do you hear me, who's the father?'

'I … couldn't say.'

Anger flashed in Josefina's eyes. 'What, is this a joke? You get knocked up while working in my house, and you won't tell me who the father is? Or you just don't know which man it could possibly be? You have some nerve—lots of nerve …' Josefina trailed off. 'When's it due?'

'The spring, I think. April.'

'That doesn't give you much time, does it? To organize yourself.'

'I have nothing to organize.'

Josefina harrumphed, 'Well, you may have to organize other employment, for one.'

Consuelo was crushed. It was what she feared the most. She closed her eyes, feeling herself start to slip down a long, black tunnel. She didn't know where it led. Josefina took pity; she relished cutting people with her tongue, but usually regretted the effects. 'Oh, well … you can work here until you get very big. I'd say you have several months. But you know yourself, Consuelo, I can't have you heavily pregnant around here. People will talk. They'll talk for sure. They'll talk no matter what, but I tell you they'll talk ferociously if I have you wandering around here with your stomach the size of a prize-winning pumpkin. Does Rogelio know?' Josefina looked at Consuelo searchingly for betrayed emotion.

'Of course not, I've only told Delaila.' Consuelo gave away nothing that Josefina could interpret one way or the other. Her radar had been successfully blocked.

'Ai … Go back to your work.'

Consuelo turned to leave. Josefina launched one last barb, 'And in future keep your legs crossed.'

Consuelo left Josefina's dressing-room to return to her chores.

'Unbelievable, just unbelievable, really. You know … Abuela Josefina has told me this tale as well—from a slightly different point of view, of course.'

Consuelo looked at me, surprised. She was in the kitchen, rolling dough for empanadas. The mincemeat filling sat bubbling on the stovetop, the scent of olives, tomatoes and beef curling up into the kitchen, adding their contribution to the dark spot on the ceiling. I sat at the table, watching her work and listening to her talk. 'She told you this? She told you my story?'

'Well, it's her story too, Consuelo. She was there, you know.'

Consuelo didn't respond directly to this, but instead asked, 'Why did she tell you my story?'

'It was in the context of a reprimand. She was trying to give me an allegorical lesson in chastity.' I smiled tightly, thinking with embarrassment and anger of the afternoon when Josefina had lectured me. Consuelo turned off the fire under the meat, and moved the pan to an unlit back burner to let the mixture cool off before she filled the pastries.

'Ok, well, I was the one who was pregnant, you know. I was the one. No her. It was no her business who the father was, and it was no her business to tell people about me.'

'But you're telling me the same story, Consuelo.'

'Is for me to tell.'

'Ok, ok—so tell me more, Consuelo. You had the baby?'

One night in April 1954, the pains started after eating the poor man's caldo Gallego her brother Joaquin made—no ham hock or flank steak—and they continued through the night. At first, Consuelo was sure it was indigestion. Joaquin was known for his vile but thrifty measure of using vegetables and meats even when they were past their prime. Joaquin called for the midwife after several hours, when Consuelo's groans became louder. The midwife examined Consuelo, checked the signs, made a small prayer, which Consuelo and her mother joined in on, and determined that it would be noon before movement of any sort could be expected. She predicted birth by the following evening. Consuelo was horrified at the thought of twenty-four hours in labor, and watched tearfully as the midwife left the yard through the unpainted wooden fence and walked down the dirt lane back towards Havana.

During the night, Consuelo tried to stay out in the yard in order not to wake the family. Her mother had sat with her for a while, but she had to be at the factory at 6 am to wash the floors and needed a few hours of sleep. Her brother did what he could, but Consuelo didn't want him around too much—this was no place for males, and they'd already caused her enough trouble anyway.

At first their affectionate, wire-haired mongrel nuzzled her hands and large belly to comfort her. Eventually, Consuelo's moaning and groaning were so loud and persistent and her tolerance to touch so slight that the dog feared approaching her, the usually pesky rooster stayed perched in the avocado tree and the goat pulled on his tether in the direction of the back of the house, away from Consuelo.

She walked to ease her pains, clutching the fence as she paced from one end of the yard to the other. Bicyclists went by, as did the neighborhood women, home from working a night in the city.

Rodriga, a prodigiously sized prostitute, walked up to the gate to chat with Consuelo. 'Your labor pains are coming the same?' She had stopped in the previous evening to check on Consuelo before heading into town for the night.

Consuelo nodded, unable to speak or draw breath as she was seized by a contraction. She grabbed onto the fence, squeezing the wood for comfort. Rodriga placed a large black hand, fingernails painted red, fake emerald ring flashing in the moonlight, on Consuelo's, squeezing the fingers and standing with her as the contraction passed and Consuelo felt relief.

Rodriga looked on Consuelo with pity. 'You know ... we could have taken care of this months ago. No one would've known. You would still have your job. I don't know why you didn't take me up on that.'

Consuelo shook her head, 'Thanks ... no ... I wanted the baby. Maybe I wanted the companionship. I don't know. I just couldn't do it.'

Rodriga shrugged and nodded. She smiled, showing a wide gap in her teeth. 'And I'm sure it will be a lovely, fat baby. A fine baby to give you support in the future. I have to go to bed for a few hours, but you come knocking if you need anything. Or send the midwife.' Rodriga gave Consuelo a kiss on the cheek before walking away down the lane. Consuelo watched her leave, feeling forlorn.

Later, Consuelo was still pacing, still having intermittent pains, still having no desire to push. She feared the midwife could be right. She steadied herself with the thought, 'It doesn't mater how much pain you have, Consuelo. The pain is part of it.'

So in addition to her pacing in the yard, Consuelo started a litany of prayers that she repeated for hours, through all her pains, her pacing, and eventually her final labor. She prayed to La Caridad del Cobre, Jesus Christo, Elegua, Oshun, Saint Barbara, in short, the lot of them. She couldn't remember who oversaw childbirth, so she decided to be better safe than sorry.

The dog lay asleep near the front door. The goat was asleep. The rooster was asleep. The chickens made no noise. The whole world seemed to be at rest except for her. She struggled and fought through the night to give birth to a living child.

It seemed not long into her painful vigil when her mother came out of the house, dressed for work and carrying a small pail with her boiled egg and banana. Stopping at the front gate, she caressed Consuelo's face.

'Take care now. The midwife will be back in a few hours. Hopefully, I'll be home in time for the birth. I look forward to seeing the baby's smiling face.' She paused a moment, as she tied her blue headscarf under her chin. 'Maybe it'll confirm once and for all who the father is. Maids have no luck, my dear. No luck at all.' She kissed Consuelo on the forehead, and headed off to work in the same direction and at the same pace as the midwife had the evening before, slow and steady, in towards Havana proper. Consuelo watched her go, her pains easing for a moment.

As predicted, it was the following evening, in the bedroom, surrounded by midwife and mother, after a protracted and painful twenty-four hours, that Consuelo gave birth to a healthy, live, big, fat, screeching, gurgling baby.

I bit into one of Consuelo's empanadas, straight out of the oven, and the steam rising from the meat at the center of the small pie burned the top of my mouth. 'Argh.' I quickly took a sip of water.

Consuelo laughed at me. 'You are being too greedy. Let it cool down.'

'I'm hungry—we haven't eaten since the waffles ... but I'll wait until it's cooled off a bit before I finish the rest of it.'

The French doors were open to allow us free conversation as Consuelo was coming in and out of the house, cleaning animal cages on the back porch. The light out back was starting to dim. The Magic Hour, they called it. Filmmakers liked the Magic Hour. I liked the Magic Hour. It took the edges off objects and people, and at the same time brought everything into painterly relief. It gave me insight that I couldn't access at other times of day. It was the perfect time to talk, to listen, to learn, to watch carefully as things from other realms would be sure to reveal themselves at this time, in this place, to me in particular.

Consuelo came inside holding a bird feeder and water bottle. She stood at the sink to clean and refill them. She was careful to ensure the birds had enough clean water and food. I watched her short, quick movements, her sure way, and her strong, experienced hands as they wiped the plastic and filled the receptacles. She went back out to put them into the cages once more. The parakeets chirped in protest. I could hear, but not see, their wings batting against the chicken wire, their little feet grasping the sides of the cage.

Consuelo spoke to the birds, 'There, that should be enough for you little ones for a coupl'a days.' She crossed the frame of the French doors and disappeared to the other side of the porch. I saw just the edge of her, bending over to retrieve a worn blanket, which she carefully placed over the birdcages. 'The rabbits don' need a blanket, they just hide in their hutches.' I nodded, having nothing to add to her discussion of animal husbandry. 'I love them, my animals. My little ones, they are totally dependent on me. Can you believe there are people in the world who treat animals bad? Animals are totally dependent on us, and we should behave right, and with love.'

'I've never even owned a budgie. But I couldn't agree with you more.' I tried the empanada again. It was a bit cooler. Consuelo finished with her animal care chores, but stayed outside. She lit a cigarette and stood on the back porch, puffing into the evening, regarding the lake with calm acceptance.

'The animals are like your babies.'

'Yes …'

'Your child, Consuelo, the child in your story just now … he lived?'

'I had a healthy boy. He was a long baby, fat and strong— large baby for a girl of my size. With great pain I bring him into this world. Over a day of labor—imagine that. These days they just give up after a few hours and slice you open and take out the baby. I'm glad I didn' have that option. Trust me, Marysol, the greater the pain, the greater the love.'

A year after the birth, Consuelo's mother was still working at the factory in the early mornings, earning steady though small wages, and her brother was a day laborer earning unsteady and small wages. Consuelo took in washing, doing it in the large tub in their yard while watching José crawl from the house to the weather-beaten wooden fence and back. By the age of one he'd made intimate friends with the dog, the goat, the neighbors, cats, migratory birds—in short anything that came into his limited sphere of existence. He was the friendliest baby she had every seen, filled with joy at the world. He only cried when extremely hungry, or if he'd hurt himself in some way, falling from the step into the yard or getting a splinter from the fence.

Consuelo thanked the Lord for José's temperament, but feared for him as well. She was worried that every day would be José's last. Would he break his head open on his adventures in the yard or in the house? Would he get a fever? Measles? Polio? Kidnapped? Would she accidentally lose him while she was taking him on her collection rounds, tied into his sling on her back while she carried loads of laundry on her front? Could he slip down and out silently, while asleep, into a sewage drain, into the hands of a witch? When he was born, she'd raced to have him baptized by the local priest, watching unflinchingly as 'bastard' was written on his birth certificate in neat and quite legible lettering.

Not long after José's first year, Consuelo received a visit. José had been playing in the yard with a black rag doll with yellow yarn hair, which his grandmother had sewn for him with an unsteady hand. Consuelo was hanging whites on the line to bleach in the sun. When she came out from behind a sheet to pick another one from the basket, she saw Miguel standing at the wooden fence, staring at the clothesline. Her heart squeezed.

'Buenos días.' He smiled broadly. José stared up at the strange man, mesmerized.

'Buenas.' She returned in kind. 'What brings you here?'

She stood, rooted to the spot.

'I wanted to see how you were getting on.' He stood uncomfortably at the gate for a moment, 'May I come in?'

'Oh, of course! Sorry.' She raised the latch on the gate and welcomed him into her home. 'I'm sorry, I don't think the place is quite, eh, organized really. There may be dirty dishes, or diapers, I don't know …'

'Don't worry about it, I don't mind..'

Consuelo scooped up José and led Miguel into the small house. It was neat and clean in the living area, though she made a point not to let him see the kitchen, which had not been attended to since the night before. Miguel sat on an old sofa, under a large, carved wooden crucifix, made by Joaquin with the help of a neighbor many years ago. Consuelo had cut, sewn and draped a tiny loincloth on the image of Jesus, and Joaquin had taken care to paint the small stigmata at the center of His palms red. Consuelo regularly took down and washed the loincloth, pounding it with her other whites, and ensuring Jesus looked at least as presentable as the other members of the family.

José reached his arms out in silent plea for Miguel to pick him up. Miguel happily lifted the child out of Consuelo's arms and placed him on his knee. He bounced José up and down gently, eliciting squeals of delight from the child.

Consuelo took the opportunity to scurry into the kitchen. 'I'll get you a coffee.'

'Thanks.'

In the kitchen, Consuelo hurried about, wiping the best cups and rooting around for any kind of cracker she could find. She could hear José laughing and Miguel neighing like a horse. She called out to Miguel from the kitchen, 'It's very nice of you to visit. It's good to see you … it's been a while. I'm sure you've been very busy.'

'I was picked up by the police. I was in jail for just a short while, then I had to lay low, leave Havana for a while.'

'Oh.' Consuelo didn't know what to say. She furrowed her brows, staring at the cafetera, wishing the boiling water Godspeed to infuse the coffee grinds, so she could return to the living-room and keep an eye on things. Should she ask him what he was in jail for? Should she leave him alone with the child?

From the other room, Miguel sensed the tension, 'For the meetings, Consuelo. Batista's men infiltrated the meeting you were at and took us in.' Porcelain clattered in the kitchen. 'Don't worry, they don't know your name. They don't know you were ever there. I didn't give a single name, not a single name, and no one else from that day knows you. You fortunately left too soon after the speech to greet anyone. At the time I was annoyed that you ran off so quickly, but now I suppose I'm happy about it.'

Miguel looked up at Consuelo as she returned to the living-room with two coffees. A tiny biscuit was perched on the edge of his saucer, the only one Consuelo had. 'You're too kind.'

'Nonsense.'

Consuelo sat at the far end of the couch, sipping her coffee. José crawled into the space between them, lying there with his cheek on the cushion and buttocks in the air, blinking away sleep.

'It's time for his nap. He takes a late morning siesta, an afternoon siesta, a siesta anytime he wants, in fact—the life, huh?' She ran her fingers gently through the child's thick black hair, brushing it back from his eyes, which were fully closed now. José started to breath heavily the baby breath of sleep where all cares are shed, if indeed they ever existed.

Consuelo and Miguel sat silently for a while, concentrating

on the coffee, and Miguel on his biscuit. The door was open and in the yard they could see the flutter of the hanging laundry against the breeze, the passage of schoolchildren in dark trousers, white shirts and red cravats, home for lunch and siesta, the dog circling the yard, looking for a comfortable spot, and dropping into a heap when he found one. The rooster, incongruously, crowed at midday.

'That's a good sign.' Miguel looked at Consuelo—she hadn't realized she'd said that aloud. There seemed to be a direct pathway from her subconscious to her vocal cords at times.

'Is it? That's good, I need one of those.' Miguel finished his coffee, put the cup down on the table in front of the sofa, and reached into his pocket. 'I've brought you a little gift.' He pulled out some pesos and a few American dollars and pressed them into her hand.

'What? What is this? No, I don't think so, Miguel, I'm sure you need this for yourself. Look, for now my family and I are eating fine.'

'Don't be silly, take this, Consuelo, take it, I'm not leaving here with it. I'll bury it in the yard or paste it to your wall, but I won't take it with me.'

'You couldn't possibly afford this. You're just out of prison, you'll need this to carry you through until you find a job, maybe you need this to support your cause ... you must have a woman who needs you, it I mean,' Consuelo looked at Miguel from the corner of her eye to see what his reaction would be to this last comment.

But Miguel didn't comment on his love life, 'I have no cause, Consuelo.' Consuelo said nothing. José slept on. 'I've renounced it. To stop the torture, I renounced it. I signed a document. Others in the jail with me, they signed the document, too. Copies were posted all over the university. The others will have nothing to do with me.' He stared at his hands. 'Between you and me, I don't expect this condition to last. The statement was made under duress, you understand. In my heart nothing changes, you know.' Miguel tried to smile, but failed.

'Torture?'

'I don't want to talk about it. Suffice to say that you don't want to see my back.'

Consuelo put a hand to her mouth in horror. But Miguel was wrong. She did want to see his back. She would look happily on it for hours on end.

'I'm sorry, Miguel. I wish there was some way I could help you hurt less. Listen, I can't take your money. You seem to need it much more than I do. Please.'

'The money isn't mine. It comes from someone else. I was given some as well. Don't worry, because the man who sent you this money isn't short of money in support of himself or his cause. He knows where my heart stands on the matter. Take the money, and don't think about it again. I'll ferry small amounts to you when I can. I don't know when that will be.' At this, Miguel took in the features of her face, and said, 'But if the money were mine I'd still insist you have it.'

Consuelo stared at Miguel's dark eyes, her will slowly melting away, sucked into his own. She could feel the organs in her body reorganizing themselves, bunching up in tension at the center of her torso, her heart squeezing blood through her vessels at breakneck speed. She tore her eyes away and looked at the baby. She thought, but did not say, 'Don't sleep with him, Consuelo. You've got enough on your plate.'

It took every ounce of will she had to say, 'Miguel, it's been good to see you. I'm sorry for what you've suffered. Let me know if I can help you to forget the ugly memories. I hope you come again soon. I hate to cut this short, but I have to finish the laundry. I have to do the colored clothing next, for a woman in town. Her maid's very sick. She needs the clothing back tonight.' She forced a smile. Consuelo knew that Miguel must feel that he was being shooed away. He must sense her nervousness.

Miguel leaned over and kissed the bottom of the sleeping baby's foot. He stood, and walked to the doorway. 'Thank you and yes, I'll certainly return. I look forward to it.' Miguel left. He walked out from the relative cool and dimness of the house into the blinding sun of midday. He let himself out of the gate, replacing the latch, and made a right turn, taking him further into the slums.

Un Premio Pa'l Heroismo

The Revolution hadn't been immediate. From the mountains into the city, from the countryside into the town, they'd advanced. Slowly winning campesinos, they'd advanced. Sweet-talking their way through cantinas, they'd advanced. From the outer provinces to the core of Havana, they'd advanced. The Revolution was, as revolutions are, a process.

In 1955 there were murmurings of change throughout the country. From Oriente to Pinar del Río people were revolting and some were worried. Consuelo believed that things would change; they couldn't stay as they were. She had grown used to it, but it seemed wrong that half the women in her barrio were prostitutes. And her neighborhood had it good. In the countryside, it was practically indentured servitude: people married their employers—but with no hope of a mention in the family will.

Consuelo was getting desperate. José was walking now, if

unsteadily. He was more independent, and consuming more food. He had learned to say 'no' to her. Over and over. Consuelo had assumed his getting older would be a good thing for her, that she'd be able to return to work, but he needed more care now than before. She half considered accepting the offer of Rodriga and the girls in her apartment to watch José in the daytimes before they went to work. But as much affection as Consuelo had for Rodriga, she didn't want to let José grow up in a household of prostitutes. She worried, however, that her resolve would not last, and she told this to Delaila, who visited from time to time, bringing pies or stews or sweets with her.

'I think Josefina would take you back.'

It was a Wednesday, Delaila's day off, and she was under the crucifix in Consuelo's living-room. Miguel was visiting as well. Delaila and he had run into each other in the front yard, as both tried to unlatch the gate. Consuelo had welcomed them inside, happy that these two could get to meet one another.

José stood by the sofa, holding onto Delaila's knees. Delaila stroked his cheeks, leaning over from time to time to plant kisses on his violet-water-scented head. She pinched his cheeks, 'I've never seen such an adorable little bundle.'

'Little—he's a giant. He's eating me out of house and home.' Consuelo smiled down at José, knowing he couldn't help it. In the last few months Miguel had been unable to secure more funds like the ones he'd given her that first day. 'Joaquin hasn't gotten work in ages—we've really got to get him some kind of a skill, but I don't know what. He's untidy, he can't cook, and he has no trade. The goat's gone, and we can't afford to buy another. The chicken coop is down to its last hen. The rooster has not been doing his job, let me tell you, Delaila. I've never known one to go through such a dry spell. The chickens are giving him the cold shoulder.' Delaila and Consuelo both giggled at this.

'Dear, I'm telling you, I think Josefina would be open, perhaps with a little persuasion, to take you back. And you could bring your child. Lord knows the place needs a bit of livening up. She never replaced you, you know, and I can't do all of the work you did in the past, I'm too old. She gives Margarita, the Machado's maid, a few pesos on her day off to cross the street to us and beat and hang the washing, and do some dusting and mending. But did I tell you? They haven't had a dinner party in months. Josefina didn't like Margarita's interaction with gentlemen visitors,' Delaila raised her brows meaningfully. 'I'm afraid I'm going to lose my touch at serving more than two people at a time if they don't organize a big party soon.'

'There are other women who need the work. They should bother themselves to look.'

'You forget what I've told you in the past about Josefina —she has a good heart. She feels guilty. Anyway, Rogelio wasn't too happy she let you go. He likes his papers ironed and everything done just so. And I always thought he liked the sight of you in your uniform.'

'Yes, well …' Consuelo blushed, 'That's not a good thing, and reminding Josefina of it won't help.'

'No, of course not.'

'Do you really want to go back there, Consuelo?' Miguel spoke up for the first time that afternoon. Consuelo thought he'd been quiet because he'd been overwhelmed by the women's talk.

'Yes. It was a good job. They paid me well. I could eat and sleep there. I've done worse. And if I could bring José …' She looked hopefully at Delaila, who was popping into her mouth one of the meringues she'd brought as a gift.

Delaila sucked on it for a while, and then answered, 'I think something can be arranged.'

And that is how Consuelo came to be standing at the Castillo front door once again, suitcase under one arm and baby in the other, waiting for a doorbell chime to be answered at about 10 am on a Thursday.

Through the door, Consuelo heard Chichi bark, the tiles creating an echo, shattering the quiet of the house. Consuelo thought to herself: 'Rogelio isn't home,' for if he had been, the dog certainly would not have been inside. She heard Chichi race and position herself just inside the front door, sounding the alarm for the household.

'Chichi, it's me. Consuelo.' The dog stopped barking. The silence was replaced by the sound of tapping heels. Consuelo was surprised. She'd assumed Delaila would answer the door.

Consuelo timed the taps. She knew by heart how many steps from sitting-room, to hallway, to front door. The taps grew louder, then ceased. The door was not opened. Josefina must have been observing her through the small pane in the front door. Consuelo couldn't see in because of the reflection of the sun, but she was sure Josefina could see out. Consuelo maintained as neutral a look as possible on her little face.

The door opened. Josefina stood there, statuesque. Her eyes lit on José. He stared back at her, reaching for her collar. She smiled ever so faintly. 'Consuelo. Entra.' Josefina stepped aside to let Consuelo enter, closed the door behind her. In the sitting-room, Josefina enthroned herself on the settee, took a cigarette out of her wood and tile cigarette box, and lit it. She did not offer one to Consuelo.

'And his name is?'

'José.'

Josefina puffed, taking this into consideration. 'Common enough name.'

'I like it.'

'Mmmm ... so, I understand, from a variety of sources, that you would like your position back, and that in addition, you would like to bring the young gentleman with you.' Josefina surveyed José, resting on Consuelo's hip, checking him out from pudgy thigh to large, dark head. 'You can put him down, he seems to be incredibly heavy.'

'He is—but I wouldn't want him upsetting your things in the room.'

'No need to worry, I'll watch his roaming ... you can put him down.'

Cautiously, Consuelo let José descend from her hip to the floor. José, as gregarious as children get, immediately started to explore, walking, as was his way, directly to Josefina, where he leaned against her knee, and stared up at her wide-eyed. Josefina stared back at him, fighting back a smile, until she could no longer do so. She grinned and pinched his cheek. 'He's adorable.' José laughed and buried his face in her pale cotton skirt. Josefina put her hands on his head.

Consuelo returned to the matter at hand, 'A variety of sources?'

'Word has come to me from a cousin of Rubén Castro that I should give you a break. That Rubén suggests so himself, and I ask myself: why does Rubén Castro care for you?'

Consuelo felt confusion and some panic, but tried not to let this show. 'Rubén Castro ... I'm not sure. Maybe he remembers me from serving at a dinner party, or I ... don't know. Isn't he in Mexico? I read in the papers ...' Consuelo's mind was spinning, but she tried to get ahold of herself. 'Who is this cousin?'

'I don't know him. A peasant on the mother's side—

something González.' Consuelo relaxed, smiling, 'Maybe you should ask why this cousin cares for me.'

'Ah. A lover … well, Consuelo, I don't have to tell you that you should take care of that, for your own sake if nothing else.' Josefina paused here and gave Consuelo a look. 'Frankly, we'd like to have you back. The washing and mending haven't been the same. I refuse to let any other street trash in here. And,' Josefina paused before adding this last bit, 'I understand you're in need. I'm sorry.' Josefina reached out to caress the child's face. José smiled at her, and with a plop dropped to the floor and started to play with one of his toes.

Consuelo, 'Thank you, Josefina, I can't tell you how much I—we—appreciate this.'

'Just one thing, Consuelo. If you get pregnant again in this house, unmarried, I can't say I'll extend the same courtesy again.'

'She hasn't changed a bit. She controls where she can.' Night had fallen. The Magic Hour had long past, but in vino veritas, and I was making do as I could with the Spanish wine we'd picked up earlier in the day. The problem, however, with plying your subject with wine, is that if you keep up copa por copa you end up in the same state yourself. We were on bottle number two of a Cencibel that I can't recall the name of.

'Is a pleasure to have you here, Marysol. It really is.' Consuelo poured herself some more wine from the bottle on the coffee table. We were in the living-room with the doors open for the breeze. The lights were off, in order not to attract too many insects, and we burned citronella candles to discourage mosquitoes. Consuelo had also lit the candle for La Virgen, who kept tabs on us from the corner, and spritzed some

White Shoulders on the statue and in the room in general because, as she explained, 'Is her favorite perfume, and me too.'

'Generally, I accept things as they are sent to me and try not to question too much—who wants to upset the saints? But I am very curious: how did you find me? I think that Josefina, she would not be too helpful in this. And I don' think anyway that she would know where I am or what I do ...'

'Let's just say it's my own personal skill. I've developed it over a few years ... Do you know how I make my money? I mean, I don't make much money ... but anyway I manage to pay the rent and I've got that great bike. I also have a beat-up little car, but I wouldn't have trusted it to take me all the way up here without a breakdown.'

'You are ... let me see ...' Consuelo scrunched her face in thought. 'Ice-cream vendor? You have a white van and you go around the streets of Miami Beach selling heladitos to little children?' She smiled, toes wiggling in delight.

I smiled at her little joke, 'No! I don't sell ice cream.'

'Ok, ok ... the zoo? You are monkey-keeper?' Giggles this time. She was having fun.

'No ...'

'Ballerina?' She laughed at this one, and I was slightly offended.

'Why is ballerina such a wild idea? Anyway, you're all over the place with these guesses, Consuelo. You're making terrible fun of me.'

'How am I supposed to guess? I have no idea. I wish I had met you years ago, but little dear, I never know you or see you until you ring me a couple of weeks ago, and then yesterday arrive to my house on that big yellow-and-black bicycle of yours. I don' know what you make money at. How do you make money?'

'I'm a journalist. I write for a paper. I investigate local interest stories.'

'Oh no, you are not going to write all of these things that we talk about here? About Rubén, and all that? Maybe he get mad at me ...' Consuelo looked truly horrified.

'No, no, don't worry—this is for my personal history. I'm not going to put you in the paper.'

Consuelo accepted this answer. 'But how did you find me? How did you know where to look?'

'I just asked. Josefina had told me lots of stories. You figured in a lot of them. But when I asked her about your whereabouts, she'd either say she didn't know, or that you'd probably stayed in Cuba. But, remember Sara and Rosa, my cousins?'

I'd made a visit to them. I'd finished college, and was kicking around South Florida, unemployed and armed with a four-year degree and a massive student loan. Sara and Rosa had found jobs. They were both secretaries with small firms. Isabella, their mother, was happy, assuming that they were finally settling down. But Sara and Rosa had just come to the realization that they would be better able to finance their partying if they had weekly paychecks. So, they systematically set about getting well-paid but not very demanding jobs, not too far from the home they still shared with their parents.

I hadn't seen them for five years, since I was a teen. In the intervening years, my Cuban accent had softened. I sounded American. I dressed differently. I'd learned things they hadn't learned and seen things that they hadn't seen and read books that they hadn't read. I was a person removed from myself. Miami was now a place I saw on television. It was a caricature of itself, revealed to me through pastiche, created in wide swathes of color. Four years in the North with only one summer in Florida had made me a stranger. I looked at everyone in the street with new eyes. I heard their accents as if I'd never heard them before—a strange music of timbales and maracas interspersed with American words. I thought that there was no way back for me. So I moved home. I packed up the books and clothes and cassette tapes, threw them into a very old and dingy Toyota and headed south.

Walking into their house was like walking into the past. The dog, Pablo, was still there, though older and slower. The kitchen appliances and counters and plates and dishes, all in varying shades of green and beige, though worse for wear, were in their expected places. The brown velour living-room couch sat in the same position, with bald patches at the corners and a few buttons missing on cushions. It was, like everything else in the neighborhood, a somewhat faded yet whole and intact memory.

I'd wished I could have said the same about my own household. Rogelio had passed away—alcoholism and a pack-a-day habit had seen to that. Josefina hung onto our world through sheer force of will, counting out her days in a nursing home I visited as often as possible. My mother and father had moved out of the two-family home into a small house in the same southwest Miami barrio. They'd taken care of Josefina as long as they could, but eventually she became too much of a handful and they'd found a local nursing home for her.

When I entered Sara and Rosa's place, my eyes watered. Visiting them and Isabella and Oscar Arnau again after my years away was the closest I could get to the past, the closest I could get to Cuba. My own family had moved at a steady pace towards Americanization, suburbanization, isolation. These Arnaus had clung onto the sixties and seventies, a place where the older generation could barely speak English, where everyone stuck together, where no one really knew what America had in store for them. They huddled together with the neighbors, bivouacked in their own little world, not realizing that America was actually a permanent encampment. Their house, their lives, reeked of the past. The look of it assaulted you. You could hug Cuba and your childhood, bring it next to you, stroke it and know that it had not left you. It was there I visited, looking, searching for the past of my past.

It was an evening, after work. Isabella was in the kitchen, hovering over the stove. She had aged well in the intervening years. She still wore high heels. She hadn't succumbed to the comfortable lace-up shoes worn by other women who had reached their zenith around the time of the Revolution. Sara and Rosa, in their work heels and little skirts and matching handbags, were splayed on the living-room couch. Isabella had let me in the front door with a flurry of kisses and hugs. When I entered the living-room where she told me the girls were, I was greeted by surprised stares. 'Baby cousin!' We exchanged kisses and I threw myself onto the couch next to them.

We spent the evening catching up. I joined the family for dinner, Oscar as quiet as ever at the head of the table, listening to all that went on around him, rarely adding a word. I told them about some of my adventures in college: staying up all night studying for exams with coffees and pizzas delivered from the 24-hour pizza place on campus; a road trip to New York City with my roommates; writing for the student newspaper; taking a bus to go on a protest in Washington DC against the war. They wondered how long before I would get paying work, and I couldn't guess. I hadn't been trying very hard. Sara and Rosa were still dating lots of men, but no one in particular appealed. Isabella was still at the make-up counter downtown. Oscar was doing layout, illustrations and graphic design for a newspaper—which is how the offer of some potential help getting my foot in the door came up. I could have gotten work in the city where I'd gone to university, but the lure of home, of securing the moorings of my emotional ropes, brought me back to Miami, a town in the process of becoming a city with only one major newspaper.

We shared gossip on our family and the neighborhood and the comings and goings of other people's children. Gladice had gotten pregnant and not long afterward married, to a very kind auto mechanic. She was living now in a neighborhood of western Miami. I said I would go visit her, knowing that I probably wouldn't. Maria taught physical education at a local primary school, and was well liked by all the students. She herself regularly entered marathons and bike races and kept active and fit, which I was glad to hear as well. She was engaged to be married to another teacher in the school.

At this point in the dinner-table conversation all eyes turned to me expectantly. 'I'm not married or engaged, nor does the possibility of either of these eventualities exist in the short to medium term.' It was my line, rehearsed for my parents.

A dark look descended like gauze on Isabella's face. It seemed that my Northern education and the possibilities that lay before me were not good enough—I didn't have a man in tow. I was disappointed to disappoint them. I wasn't thrilled about this either, but I couldn't change the way things stood at that moment.

Isabella's face brightened, 'We'll help to find you a man. There are lots of nice men at the newspaper.'

'Thanks, Tia Isabella, but I'm ok. I'm in no hurry. And marriage—I don't see why I need to go down that path just yet. Or ever.' I expected comments to the contrary, especially from Oscar—the quiet, serious authoritarian who never said much, and when he did, it was uttered in the form of decree. He said, 'You're quite right in this approach.'

Isabella, Sara and Rosa gave him a surprised look.

He continued, 'I think it's best for Marysol. I'm not saying it's the best way for everyone, but it seems to suit her.'

A partial victory for the Castillo and Arnau women was achieved at the dinner table that evening.

Later, Sara, Rosa and I were sitting on Sara's bed, looking through old photographs she kept neatly in a bound book and chatting. We found a family picture of a group on the front lawn of my house. 'And the little baby in Josefina's arms is you, Marysol. Your dad is looking tall and handsome, and your mom, Luz, very slim. I don't know who that lady is, though,' Rosa looked quizzically at the woman at the end in the faux Pucci dress.

I took a good look, and recognition of the old woman in the much younger face dawned, 'Oh, I think that's the woman from across the street. A very young Gabriella Guzman, Gladice's mother.'

We continued to flip through photographs, moving in reverse chronological order until we reached Cuban photographs, brought to Florida in batches with the different waves of our family's political refugees, each group smuggling out meaningful shards of their lives in pieces that would fit in the suitcases on the plane, or under the inserts of their shoes. Josefina had sewn her engagement and wedding bands into the lining of her brassière. She had panicked when she heard that she was going to be strip-searched, and had nearly thrown the bra into the garbage. But Rogelio, keeping presence of mind, snatched it just in time and stuffed it into the crotch of his pants. They passed over him for the strip search.

We came across a picture of Abuela and Abuelo's staff, lined up neatly on the lawn. There was a large, old woman in a floor-length skirt and apron, obviously the cook. She seemed out of place in this photo taken in the 1950s, like someone had clipped her out of one taken in 1910 and pasted her in. There was a thin black man, who Sara explained did the gardening but only visited the premises once a week or so. There was a small, shapely woman in neat white uniform and frilly apron standing at the end of the group and slightly in front of the other two. This woman showed up again in other photos—she was in the background at parties; she stood holding a baby, holding a dog, and in one, a picture of Josefina while she was at her vanity table, the woman stood holding a fox stole, as Josefina prepared to let it be placed on her shoulders so she could secure it with a shiny clasp.

'Who's the small one?'

'That's Consuelo,' Sara said.

'Oh, Consuelo! I've never seen her before—she certainly features in a lot of the stories in our family. I've heard that name again and again, but I've never seen her. She seemed important to Abuela Josefina. She was at so many family events.'

'Yeah ...' Rosa looked at me, smiling sadly.

'What happened to her? I mean, where is she? Didn't they bring her with them when they came?'

'Are you kidding?' Sara snorted. She lit a cigarette, as did Rosa. They offered one to me, and I took it. After years of having everyone I knew smoking around me constantly, it had finally rubbed off. 'By the time the Castillos fled Cuba, Consuelo was long gone. She'd become part of La Revolución, didn't you know?'

'No, how would I know? All the stories I've heard from Abuela end just before the Revolution. I've asked, I've wanted to know about the time afterwards … but it's a fog. As far as I know Cuba was discovered in 1492 by Christopher Columbus, continued on a prosperous and upward trajectory until 1959—and then nothing. Their history seems to emerge from the mist when they come to Miami in 1968.'

'Well, Josefina and Rogelio, you know, they still imagine themselves to be at the height of their beauty, their wealth, their strength, everything. Well, imagined, God rest Rogelio's soul,' we all crossed ourselves. 'They never really faced reality.' Sara sounded bitter.

There was a definite divide between Oscar and Isabella's family, the Arnaus; and Rogelio and Josefina's, the Castillos. Oscar, though of the same stock as Josefina, had always been more of a proletariat. He was the outsider, the artist, the supporter of the workingman. Josefina had in many ways lived up to her heritage. She wore her elitism like a painted scarf wrapped loosely around her throat. But there was something in her that set her apart from her bourgeois neighbors and classmates—some unearthed sentiment, some tendency towards the dramatic or the literary, which bore witness to the genetic link shared with Oscar.

'Marysol,' Rosa dragged deeply on her cigarette before continuing, 'Josefina and Rogelio stood in lines for rations like the rest of our families. Like the rest of Havana and Santiago de Cuba and Cienfuegos and Santa Clara. They starved, scratched and were sent to the fields like the rest of them.'

'They were sent to the fields?'

'Fields, my girl. It was like what they did in Russia … what do you call them?'

'Gulags? Labor camps?'

'Yes. You've read a lot, haven't you read Cuban history? Haven't you heard of them?'

'Well, there's not much written on them. I know of them, have heard vague mentions from people, but I didn't know we'd been part of that. Abuela never told me she was in one of those.'

'Well, it wasn't supposed to be punishment, but it was. It was for Patria. As part of the application for an exit visa, those healthy enough had to serve time in the camps. It was part of their "voluntary" work scheme.' She harrumphed, 'As if Cubans could avoid volunteering. But she wasn't tortured. Say what you want, Marysol, that whole thing, it was the great leveler. Josefina cut cane like my father and mother cut cane. Like the guajiros had cut cane. Twelve hours a day, six days a week—ok? They cut it until their hands bled, they smelled of it, had the constant taste of it in their mouths, and would see it in their dreams. And it is nothing less than what everyone else did. What every campesino had been doing for centuries,' her voice went up an octave, 'They worked. They worked the way Consuelo had worked, and Miguel had worked, and everyone.'

'When? Where? I don't know anything about this.'

Sara took a drag of her cigarette, 'Well, Josefina has told our family some stories.'

It wasn't that Josefina and Rogelio had been on the wrong side of the Revolution. In fact, it was that they were on no side. They'd been disgusted by Batista, his ham-fisted approach and corruption. They hated the gangsters who were more welcomed on the island than they were. And, anyway, Batista wouldn't have been allowed into the Castillo's country club—he wasn't white enough.

But they didn't support the revolutionaries either. They thought nothing but trouble could follow that bunch down from the mountains. Josefina knew the Castro family well.

Their father had been a clever, violent bull. The cook, a grasping old cow, had fathered Rubén, Fidel and three others. Fidel was smart, but there was an edge of madness about him. He was a supreme risk-taker. Rubén might temper him, but Rogelio thought Rubén would only make Fidel lean farther to the left. The only thing that piqued their interest was Castro's promise to restore the constitution.

Josefina and Rogelio did not go out into the streets on 8 January and cheer Fidel's arrival in Havana. Neither did they participate in any anti-revolutionary violence. A sort of political paralysis settled over them, which they were never able to shake, not even in Miami. They witnessed many of their friends: doctors, lawyers, businessmen and journalists, leave and never return. Neighbors left with the contents of a suitcase. Homes stood unoccupied by humans but filled with furniture, art, clothes and books. Whole neighborhoods became like museums after closing time.

Then the revolutionaries moved in, seizing properties, turning them into government departments, apartment complexes for the poor, public institutions. Increasingly the Castillos were isolated in their small but luxurious Vadado house, a spit of dry land surrounded by rising flood waters.

In 1963, their farm in Santa Clara was seized as well as one of their bank accounts—the one with the most money. Josefina cried and cried to Oscar and Isabella to help her, but there was nothing they could do. It was needed 'for the people'. This alone, however, was not enough to either wake Josefina and Rogelio from their paralysis, nor to make them leave.

The outlawing of religion and the banning of Santa Claus affected Josefina and Rogelio more than other things. They hated the food rations, the standing in lines and waiting with ration books, but the banning of religion put fear in their hearts. They became convinced that Fidel was the anti-Christ. They knew they had to get out even before the government started to rotate blackouts in order to conserve electricity, but it took them years to get up the courage to do so.

Josefina tried to sell her dresses and shoes for food, but no one wanted them, could afford them, or saw the need for them now that the casinos were closed. Rogelio was reassigned to driving a truck. He started a market garden in the back yard. Consuelo had joined the Revolution, and José, like all children at the time, had been sent to a children's indoctrination camp in Villa Clara.

When they hadn't been able to pay her wages any longer, Delaila had left, too. Josefina started baking birthday cakes to support herself and Rogelio. Delaila had been kind enough to come over one afternoon and show Josefina how to use her own cooking equipment. Josefina had gotten flour and egg whites all over the kitchen floor. Her first cake had emerged from the oven as a gooey, caramelized black mess. But by the third attempt, she realized, for the first time in her life, that she might actually be developing a skill that she could turn to profit. She made birthday cakes for friends far and wide. They would give her their flour, sugar and egg rations, she would scrounge up some cocoa and cream and produce fantastic creations which, in defiance of the laws of mathematics, were greater than the sum total of their ingredients.

Then all forms of private industry had been banned. Josefina and Rogelio were at a loss as to what to do. They just had not been political enough to flee earlier. They refused to attach themselves to the communists. Ricardo and Barbara had left Cuba in 1962, and had since been begging Josefina and Rogelio to join them. They saw no further reason for delay.

They applied for exit visas and airplane tickets to Miami

in the summer of 1967. Their last bank account was seized and their house was expropriated when they left the island. They were forced to leave behind the artifacts of their lives: Lladro figurines, Baccarat glass, paintings, furniture, the piano. And Josefina was forced to work in exchange for leaving the country. Rogelio was given an exemption, as he had arthritis, and had served in the armed forces for a time early during the Grau presidency. Josefina was sent to a labor camp, as many others were, as retribution for wanting to leave the country.

The bus arrived in the early morning, pulling up in front of their house in the Vedado. Josefina had been watching for it from the sitting-room, a coffee in one hand and a cigarette in the other. Rogelio had asked her to wake him before she left, but now that the moment had come, she couldn't face him to say goodbye. She was afraid she might cry.

There was a knock at the door. She exited the house quietly, not glancing up at the woman in ill-fitting fatigues who had come to collect her, her small bag containing a few personal items and work clothes slung over her shoulder. She had no idea what to expect, and when she boarded the bus, was pleased to discover that it was all women. The camps were segregated. She breathed a little easier. She chose a seat by a young, nervous looking blonde girl with blue eyes.

There was absolute silence on the bus, broken only by the occasional cough. She stared out the window at the retreating city. She didn't know where they were headed, only that she would be going to the center or east of the country, instead of west to the tobacco farms in Pinar del Río. She had no idea what she could expect when she got there, where she would be staying or what she would do.

She was frightened. Compounding the fact that she was being sent to do hard labor was that she had never, ever in her entire life been anywhere on her own. Frightened isn't the accurate word—she was panicked. She held it in, however, keeping herself together, maintaining a composed look on her face and in her eyes. Not letting them dart around as she desperately wanted to do, not grabbing the girl next to her and demanding what, if anything, she knew about where they were going, not shouting at the top of her lungs to everyone on the bus (including the sort of female kapo they had sitting at the front), 'This is not fair!' She sat quietly, looking out the window: now at the sea, now at the countryside, now at men on horses, now at men with rifles, now at men in fatigues, now at women bicycling along a dirt road.

They passed Matanzas and went through Jovellanos, where the Parque Central and church inflicted on her a stabbing memory of Santiago de Cuba. She fell asleep after that for a while, she wasn't sure for how long, and woke to early afternoon sun. She'd slept through the rest stop and had to go to the bathroom, but the woman in the fatigues told her that she would have to wait.

So Josefina stared out the window again. It wasn't long before the countryside became terribly familiar. She was near Santa Clara. They passed the outskirts of the town, her delicate head swiveling to see the University disappear from view behind her. The bus turned down a paved road, then a dirt road. She sat enveloped in horror as the bus pulled into the long driveway that lead up to her family estate, which she had inherited from her mother and had passed on to Rogelio to administrate. Her estate. Her land. Her cane. Her mangos. Her peasants. They now belonged to the Cuban people. Above the entrance gate, instead of 'Castillo y Arnau' written in gold wrought iron, a crudely painted placard read 'Campo 26 de Julio'.

The bus pulled up in front of Josefina's house. She got off

the bus, lining up behind the other women, and was led through her front door and into her main reception hall. Some of her same furniture was in the room, pressed into the service of the camp commanders; but most of their possessions were gone. The house was now being used as an administrative facility and lodging for the camp commanders and overseers.

Her feelings of horror receded into numbness as she stood for two hours, being processed with the other women. At one point, she was escorted to the lavatory and was watched as she used the toilet—the same toilet where she'd miscarried nineteen years earlier. She noticed that it had been stripped bare of the humorous posters she had hung in wooden frames, the outlines clearly visible on the walls: small, square, clean areas of pink paint. Ornate glass bottles of powder and bubble bath that she had brought back from her honeymoon in Spain were long gone. She pulled up her trousers and was taken back to wait in the line.

'Papers please, ladies.' Then the questions: name, address, age, height, weight, date of last medical examination, work experience. They dug through the possessions in her bag and confiscated a small bottle of perfume. She winced as they did this. When she was done at the first station, she went into another, shorter line for cursory medical examinations. It didn't take too long and, for once on that day, she didn't feel humiliated.

After the processing was over the women were each issued with army fatigues. They were marched in straight lines across the lawn and towards the old peasant bohíos in the distance. Josefina, who had been trying to remain composed for the entire day, closed her eyes in order to fight back tears. She couldn't believe that they would be accommodated in the peasant huts. When she opened her eyes again, she realized that the women were actually being led past the bohíos and towards a new, low barracks that she hadn't noticed before. It was located between the house and the huts, in the direction of the mango groves.

They were ushered inside, and there she saw a large room with camp beds lined up against both walls. There were bars on the windows. At the foot of each bed was a small, metal box where everyone could keep their possessions. The beds were assigned alphabetically, and therefore Josefina was on the left, about a third of the way down. After they put their few articles in their respective boxes, the women were led out again and shown the toilet and bathing facilities. The toilets were located in wooden outhouses, behind the building. The smell coming from them was repulsive, but not as bad as she had feared. The showers were behind the dormitory in an open, concrete area. She would have to shower communally outdoors.

After becoming acquainted with their new accommodation, the dinner hour arrived. The women were taken to another low building and each one was served a bowl of beans and rice.

That first night after the Compañera turned out the lights, Josefina lay in bed staring at the ceiling for a long time. Her mind was blank. She did not think of Rogelio. She did not think of her mother. A small smile did, however, spread slowly across her face as the irony of the situation finally became apparent to her and overcame the sense of horror she'd been experiencing until then. She fell asleep.

The next morning, the women were given bread and coffee and were marched out to the sugar-cane fields. Josefina had been to them in the past, but she had never actually touched a sugar-cane, unless it was a small chunk to chew on. The women started by learning to use a machete and efficiently chop the cane stalks. Josefina was in fear for her life, lest she should chop her own leg off, or worse, someone else's.

Around her, the same expression was crossing most of these women's faces—fear. For the first time since she'd gotten on the bus yesterday, Josefina took a good look at the other women. Their skin colors and social positions prior to the Revolution were mixed, but one thing was clear—most of these women were city dwellers and had never wielded farm implements before; some had never even been on a farm. Josefina did have the advantage of knowing, theoretically at least, the basic principles of reaping a sugar-cane harvest. The Cuban government was getting desperate, however, to improve crop production, which had fallen since the overthrow of Batista, and rotated workers out from the city to cut sugar cane—the most important crop in the country.

After the brief lesson was over, the women set to cutting cane alongside some workers who were experienced at the harvest. They moved, bent over, slowly through the fields in silence. The only sound was that of the machetes cutting through the stalks, and that of heavy breathing. Josefina had a white scarf wrapped around her head to hold her hair back and protect her scalp from the sun. Rivulets of perspiration were emerging from her hairline and tracing a track through the dust on her face down her neck to her collarbone.

Progress was unbelievably slow in the beginning: Josefina, having watched her peasants cut cane properly, knew this. Being healthy and fit, she thought that the work would be hard but manageable. She was horrified to discover that within an hour she'd developed blisters on her right hand despite the thick gloves. She switched the machete to her left hand and her progress slowed significantly. Then, an hour later, that one had blisters, too. At the midday break, she removed her gloves and took a good look at her hands, both of which were raw. She still had red paint on the nails, and it looked incongruous against the blisters, pink flesh and bleeding cracks on her palms. There was nothing alabaster about her hands now.

She trudged slowly to the edge of the field with the other women in order to get ham, bread and juice and sit under the shade of some trees. She noticed the blonde, blue-eyed girl from the day before near her. A tear was rolling down one pale check even as she chewed on her lunch. Josefina smiled at her and patted her on the knee, trying to comfort her. The girl swallowed her food and smiled back, but couldn't sustain the expression for long before she bowed her head and said, 'Six months.' Josefina looked away.

'Six months of forced labor, not all of it cutting sugar cane, she also sowed vegetable seeds, that kind of thing. And she planted pine saplings. Castro had this idea that if they grew pine trees around the coastlines it would perform as a sort of buffer against hurricane-force winds. I don't know if it worked or not. I think he gave up on it after a while.' Sara stubbed her cigarette out, and started to dig through her old LP collection for something to listen to, 'How about Styx? Tom Petty and the Heartbreakers?'

I was concentrating on this new information, 'Yeah, whatever.' I started to chew my nails, my desperate old habit, picked up during long sessions when Josefina was lecturing me. I was always having these little bombs of information dropped on me. Some family member would choose otherwise benign moments when they thought I was ready, most receptive, and they would just lay it on me. I suppose it was no less than what I deserved for my constant prying. 'That is fucking horrifying, girls.'

Rosa smiled at me, realizing that I was unhappy about

learning this about my grandmother. 'Well, it wasn't exactly Nazi Germany. I mean, they fed them and they even got weekend furloughs if they met their quota.'

'Really? That's great.'

Sara put the record on the turntable, 'But Josefina never met her quota.' Rosa gave Sara a sharp look.

'Oh.' I had to change the subject away from Josefina, 'So, what did Consuelo do for the Revolution? Did she cut cane, too. And is she here? Is she in Miami?'

A grainy, dusty-sounding Styx started playing.

'She's not in Miami, but she is in Florida.' Rosa started digging through Sara's clothes in the closet, looking for something to wear out that evening.

'Where?'

'Lakeland.'

'Do you know where, specifically? I mean, Lakeland, there's lots of people there.'

'We have the address. She wrote Josefina and Rogelio and us letters, years ago. She knew Dad from her work in the Revolution, and tried to keep in touch with him. I think the letters all went unanswered and she must have given up after a while.' Rosa pulled out a Diane Von Furstenburg dress they'd recently pooled their resources to buy. 'I'm wearing this one.'

'You're not wearing that one, I'm wearing that one.'

'You can't wear this again—you wore it last week. Give it a rest.' Rosa and Sara fought over who would wear the dress for another minute or two, Sara finally giving in to Rosa and deciding that she would wear jeans.

'Can I have it?'

Rosa looked annoyed. 'The dress? I'm wearing it.'

'No—the address. I want Consuelo's address. I want to meet her.'

Rosa and Sara looked at each other intently without speaking. Finally, Sara spoke, 'She deserves to know.'

'What do I deserve to know?'

Sara completed her thought, 'You deserve to know her, Consuelo. You deserve to meet her, why not? Just because Josefina didn't want to have anything to do with her once they were in the States doesn't mean that you shouldn't. You're an adult now and Josefina doesn't have to know … Consuelo is an important part of the Castillo history. And no, she didn't cut cane. She did some administrative work. She was taught how to handle a weapon and was given a uniform, but in the end her main job was to check people's papers as they stood in line for rations. Not very exciting. Come back for the address tomorrow. I'm going to have to dig through some boxes in the spare room here.'

'Ok, I'll be by tomorrow evening.' I got up to leave, stabbing out my cigarette.

'Want to go out with us?'

I thought about it for a moment, the night stretching ahead of me, and the day tomorrow when I had nothing to do. I took another cigarette from Rosa's pack and struck a match, inhaling Virginia tobacco. 'No, thanks. I'm just exhausted.'

Además De Paz Y Prosperidad

The rest of 1955 and 1956 came and went, a troubled year for many. In Santiago de Cuba uprisings energized campesinos, and set Batista nerves on edge. All were briefly panicked by the assassination of some government officials. Batista escaped unhurt.

But in the Castillo household there was a brief respite of bliss. Consuelo had slipped back into her routine and her duties as if there had not been an intervening year-and-a-half absence. Rogelio had his newspapers ironed well, so that they showed no creases across any text or photos, and were ready for him on the dining table in the mornings. Josefina's clothes were in constant party-ready condition, her shoes gleaming, her baths drawn to the right temperature, the sitting-room a dust-free haven for any afternoon visitors or late-night vigils.

José was the perfect complement to the household. There were none who did not love him. José possessed the rare talent of being able to bring a smile to Rogelio's face before he'd had his morning coffee. There was no shortage of food for him, as Delaila could not help but constantly feed him scraps, like one would a particularly well-behaved lap dog. He was growing fat, and contrary to Consuelo's instincts—which were to eat as much as possible in times of plenty for surely a time of want was just around the corner—she had to beg Delaila to hold back a little on the pork rinds, cakes and pastries.

But there was one reaction that mattered to Consuelo above all others. One reaction that could spell the end of her working days in the household if it was not a positive one: Josefina's. And it was a good one. Consuelo had thought that the bitterness of all of Josefina's previous miscarriages would overwhelm the household like a tidal wave and José would drown. But in fact, he floated, swam, and sailed into Josefina's good graces, in fact, her love. Consuelo made a mental note to never underestimate the production of goodwill that could be generated by a particularly well-behaved, charming and attractive baby boy.

As before, Consuelo was busy morning to night with chores. She took José into the back yard with her when she washed and hung laundry and let him play in the grass and sun. He grew brown, and he grew to be best friends with an ageing Chichi. He napped in the dining-room when she polished silver. When she dusted, though, wandering through the house taking care not to fumble with the Castillos' expensive items, she had to leave him behind. And it was during one such expedition through the house, as Consuelo was dusting vases and rearranging silver picture frames holding images of Spaniards in long dresses and pointed beards, that Josefina offered to watch José while Consuelo dusted.

Delaila was busy preparing food for the evening, with hot bubbling substances on the stovetop and open flames in the hearth. Consuelo wouldn't leave José in there. And she tried not to depend too much on Delaila, who was old, and whose movements were slow. Consuelo agreed to Josefina's suggestion, thinking to herself: 'She's young enough, she loves him, and she certainly has enough time on her hands.' She smiled as Josefina lifted the child with some difficulty into her arms, and walked off to the laundry-room in order to find his shoes and get his hat, as she intended taking him to the zoo.

The rest of the day, Consuelo was able to concentrate on her dusting. She was hoping that a thorough job on a Wednesday would mean she wouldn't have to revisit the task until the following Monday. When she was done, she changed the sheets on the guest beds (the Castillos expected some visitors that weekend), helped Delaila in the kitchen, soaked the whites out back in lemon juice and water for pounding the following day, set the table for the evening, cut fresh pink roses from the garden, and arranged them in a vase on the dinner table. She had not had this productive a day since before she'd had José. Having Josefina take care of him for the day was like removing a 28-pound ball and chain from her ankles.

Satisfied with her day's work, and not on duty again until serving the evening meal, Consuelo wandered into the sitting-room and stared at the door to the main hall, wondering when her son, and her employer, would return home. She sat in the chair for thirty minutes or more, staring at the open door, not moving, not talking, not looking at a book or magazine. The hallway was lit from a high transom window over the door and the light was reflected by the gilt-edged mirror over the hall table. Consuelo felt the cool of the caramel-colored marble in the hall floor wrap around her face like a cotton terry towel, wet and soothing.

She stared at the sitting-room door a bit more, and then, for the first time ever, carefully opened and reached into Josefina's smoking box. She ensured the box was neither very full nor very empty, and removed one Partaga cigarette. She lit it using the matches she carried in her apron pocket and inhaled deeply. She extinguished the match between thumb and forefinger, and put it, blackened, back into another pocket in her apron. She wasn't much of a smoker, yet, but she smoked on occasion, such as on Saturday nights after dinner and mornings after coffee.

The Partaga had a delicate flavor to it, different from the cheap hand-rolled cigarettes her brother made for her. Her lungs did not feel assaulted by its smoke. She felt an immediate rush of nicotine. She leaned back into Josefina's favorite chair and smoked her cigarette, slowly and deliberately and with pleasure, until it was nothing more than a nub between her fingers. She stared out at the Havana Vedado in the late afternoon.

When they finally got back that evening, José's head was lolling on Josefina's shoulder from exhaustion. Consuelo was in the sitting-room fluffing pillows. She looked up when she heard the front door open and Josefina coming into the house with slower, heavier steps than usual. They entered the sitting-room and Consuelo saw José knocked out in Josefina's arms. He'd obviously missed his nap.

José was wearing a new little sailor-boy outfit with a matching silk and wool mix hat and a new pair of white shoes. 'Josefina, you shouldn't have bothered, that's so kind of you.' Consuelo fingered the cotton of the sailor-boy pants.

'It wasn't a bother to me. This was nothing, really.' As she finished speaking, Consuelo heard the door being opened again and the sound of bags and the crinkle of paper in the hall. Rogelio's driver appeared in the doorway, his arms loaded with bags and parcels. A giant, stuffed giraffe head poked out of one paper bag; a New York Yankees' baseball pennant waved out of the top of another.

'Where shall I put these, Señora?'

'Oh, thank you Román. Please put them in the first guest bedroom, just off the hall.'

Román smiled, nodded, and went down the hallway to find the bedrooms.

'Josefina …'

'Now don't say a thing, Consuelo. It was my pleasure, all of it. Really, he's a lovely child. He's in our household now, and I'd like to treat him from time to time, if possible. There are a lot of bags I've brought home. I'll leave them in the first guest bedroom for now, and I'll just go through them and separate my things from his and then I'll show you some little gifts for him. Yes? And I was thinking … it must be cramped in that laundry-room for the two of you. It looked cramped anyway. I hadn't really seen it before. Anyway, I was thinking maybe you two could move into one of the guest bedrooms? The smaller one, near the back. It will give you more room, and you'll be more comfortable. We'll have to move some things out, of course. Anyway, perhaps you can attend to that tomorrow.'

Consuelo smiled, wondering what had gotten into Josefina. She looked like she was on some sort of high, like people she'd seen snorting cocaine and talking a mile a minute. 'Josefina, I'm indebted to you in more ways than one. You're very kind.' Consuelo looked at José's sleepy, pudgy face. 'And he looks exhausted. Hand him here, I want to put him down … hmmm, maybe I should wake him to feed him first and put him to bed for the night …' Transfer of baby was made from Josefina to Consuelo without a hitch, and José slept on, none the wiser.

'Oh, I wouldn't bother feeding him another morsel, Consuelo. He ate nearly as much as me today. We had ice creams at the zoo, and then afterwards I took him to the Yacht Club, we were just chatting with some friends of mine there, Mercedes and some girls, and we all got red beans and rice, Puerto Rican style. Then there was all the shopping, which really wore us both out, and then I got him a little bocadito. I'd say he's fueled up for two days.'

Consuelo stared at José, amazed that such a little thing could consume so many calories. 'He's going to turn into a rhino.'

'Oh, I wouldn't worry about it. Soon all that baby fat will turn into height.' Josefina patted José's cheek. She smiled at Consuelo, and left the room. A few steps down the hallway she turned back to put her head into the sitting-room, 'By the way, we have an extra person for dinner tonight. Please set another place at the table, and ensure Delaila has enough food—'

'She always has too much food.'

'Well, ensure she has enough food anyway, and maybe put on the pink uniform if you would, I like that one.' Josefina left the room again, tapping confidently away.

Josefina's first task as babysitter had not seemed to put her off, and on many occasions after that, she offered to take the child off of Consuelo's hands. José became a regular at canasta afternoons, ladies' luncheons, the shops, the parks, the playgrounds, others' houses—in short, there was nowhere Josefina wouldn't take him, and José was given entrée to a world Consuelo could only serve.

Pues Somos Soldados

Cuba as, technically, a subtropical country, does not have great swings in weather conditions from season to season. The winters in Havana can have a nip in the air and you might even need a sweater at times. The summers are the converse, and quite hot, though not as desperately hot as you might imagine—it never really goes over 90. However, in the crowded city of Havana, the summer can feel oppressive.

Oscar used to send Isabella and her sisters and nephews to a house on Varadero Beach that he would rent from June to August. He would join them on the weekends after a long week at work. Of course, that was before he got involved with the revolutionaries, and left Isabella to fend for herself for months on end. During that period she did not rent a beach house. In fact she sold her own house and moved in with her mother and sisters to ride out the storm until her husband came back to his senses, as she considered it. She waited for him to call round to collect her at any moment so that they could go back to Miramar, find a new home for themselves and rebuild what, she thought, he had managed to destroy. I can see her face in her Miami kitchen now, 'Why couldn't he have gotten a normal mistress like any other man, and not taken up a political one?'

Rogelio and Josefina often followed the same pattern during the summers, sometimes alternating beaches. The summer of 1957 was hot and the city was stuffy. Josefina didn't like what she was reading in the papers. It had been years since she had seen her brother Ricardo and her sister-in-law in Santiago de Cuba, when she'd lost her hair. She knew that the rebels were reported to be in the mountains, but she didn't find this discouraging. She didn't care much about missing Rogelio the whole summer, nor he her. So, in late May of that year, Josefina rented a house overlooking the sea, backing onto the Sierra Maestra, near her brother's house.

Consuelo agreed to go with José, whom she thought would benefit from the sea air. Delaila was left behind to cook for Rogelio on the evenings when he would be home. Josefina guessed that these would not be many. She hired in the Machado's maid again on her days off. In the years since Consuelo's absence and return, when Josefina had last brought Margarita in to clean, Margarita had fallen ill with pox. Her face had been ravaged, and Josefina now could not care less how much time she spent in the same house with Rogelio.

In 1952, when Josefina had last visited Santiago de Cuba, she'd taken a train. This time, she had a car she'd made Rogelio buy her the previous year. Nevertheless, Rogelio still sent his driver to get her for shopping expeditions and other such excursions and insisted that she drive the car as little as possible herself. He had not been able to dissuade her from taking the car to Santiago de Cuba.

Josefina was, and remained until my parents wrenched the driver's license out of her hands in my teen years, a terrible driver. When she paid attention to the road, she was fine. But she would inevitably get bored staring at the road and concentrating on the lights, other cars, animals in the road, and pedestrians. She would light a cigarette and hang her arm out the window, looking at the scenery. Most disturbing was her habit of telling stories and, inevitably, using her hands and arms to elaborate on incidents and to make her point, thereby letting go of the steering wheel. Her arm would go flailing into the passenger's side of the seat, nearly knocking someone on the nose; she would lose control of the wheel for a moment; the car would make a sincere effort to go off the road and knock itself into a palm tree or a wagon full of melons, but just at the last moment before disaster struck, she would grab hold of the wheel again, right the car, and head off. Thirty minutes or an hour would pass before she got into an impassioned discussion again and another near accident would occur. They proceeded on their journey in this fashion until they made their first stop.

They first stopped in Santa Clara on the way to Santiago. They were breaking their journey into three legs, the second one stopping in Camagüey. Josefina had not been back to the farm in years. Rogelio occasionally made visits to check in on the property and ensure the business was running well. The farm had followed Josefina into the marriage as her inheritance from her mother, but she had happily handed over every shred of responsibility to Rogelio by 1954. Her heart had gone out of it—and she had never been that interested in the business details that concerned growing and selling sugar cane or mangos. She'd also grown suspicious of the peasants, and had thought the overseer was trying to poison her.

They'd arrived at the farm in the late afternoon. Consuelo had a tough time with the key in the front door but eventually it opened. She lifted the sheets from a few pieces of furniture and threw open the shutters to see that the house had been invaded by dust motes and dead flies. She was concerned about the amount of cleaning the place needed, but Josefina told her not to bother—they'd be gone at dawn.

Consuelo put José to bed. Sipping from glasses of rum and Coke that Consuelo had prepared, they wandered about the garden behind the house, and around the wide yard to the front. Peasants had been hired to maintain these, and Josefina found them neat and pleasant, just as she remembered them.

'It's been a while, hasn't it, Consuelo?'

'Yes. The gardens look well.'

'I remember the gardens in the mornings, still dewy and the grass wet if you came out early enough, before the sun burned it all away. I remember the smell of the cane when we cut it.'

'Yes.'

'And the mangos. When they were under the trees, fallen from the branches and ripe—they smelled so sweet. They were intoxicating. They were irresistible like that.' Josefina laughed a little, 'Remember the time I found you and those two peasants under the tree, sucking at mango skins and pits, your faces covered in pulp, your fingers dripping? You were a mess. I always thought you were neater than that because you keep the house so well. You should have brought a towel with you.'

Consuelo smiled, 'The urge overcame us when we saw them ripe like that, I couldn't be bothered to run back to the house for a towel. I washed my hands and face in the stream afterwards.'

The sun, soon to be a memory, sank behind the empty stables. Consuelo decided to go to bed early with José. She would perhaps do some sewing by the last of the sun and candlelight, the electricity having been shut off. Josefina decided to stay out on the patio, 'tempting fate'. 'Don't worry,' she thought to herself, 'lightning doesn't strike twice.' There were no workers to be seen now, at dusk. No overseer. There was silence from the stables—the horses were long gone, sold at auction years ago. She hadn't wanted to ride in years. The overseer kept his stallion at the side of his house. As dark took a firm grip on the countryside, and the industrious sounds of daytime faded, nature turned up the volume on the night sounds of owls and cicadas.

In the distance, at the edges of the property, Josefina could just make out the peasant huts and lean-tos. Oil lamps were lit first in one hut and then another across the horizon. She tried to see a pattern in their appearance but couldn't find one. She heard the lowing of the cows being milked for the evening. She lit a cigarette, wondering if the faint glow of her tobacco was visible from the huts, if they were watching her. If they thought she offered some sort of communication, her cigarette sending Morse signals.

She finished her drink, putting the glass down on the patio floor and then sitting on the concrete herself. The wrought-iron furniture had been put away summers ago. When she finished one cigarette, she immediately lit another, her only form of insecticide. After a while, she heard chanting. She could discern that there were words being spoken, but she didn't know what they were. The vowel and consonant groupings sounded Spanish, but she couldn't put them together into a comprehensible whole. Drumming started. Then maracas. Clapping. Perhaps a guitar was being plucked, but she may have been imagining this. Fifteen or twenty minutes passed in this way, Josefina listening to the peasants at their ritual.

Then they started a tune she recognized. She did hear a guitar, faintly. Their voices drifted over the fields. They sang in Spanish now, forming words from her childhood,

> Me voy al transbordador
> A descargar la carreta
> Para cumplir con la meta
> De mi penosa labor
> A caballo vamo' pa'l monte

Closing her eyes, she sang along, '... vamo' pa'l monte.'

The song faded out as it had faded in, as if she were using a tuner on a radio. They started up another song, which she vaguely recognized, but to which she didn't know the words. She finished her cigarette, smashed it into the dirt under her sandal, and went inside to rest for the long trip ahead of them the next day.

Consuelo arrived at the eastern end of the island, after almost three days on the road with Josefina, completely frazzled. She'd seen her life pass before her eyes about seven times, and had been convinced that José would never make it to manhood. Josefina never took notice of her errors on the road, and arrived completely refreshed, exclaiming, 'Aaah, that was so much better than the train or even an airplane. No one to bother us, we can open the windows when we want. Stop, go, as we like. Drink wine along the way whenever the notion strikes us to open a bottle.'

Consuelo, astounded at the lack of self-knowledge this statement expressed, could only nod, her brows screwed together in worry: for, eventually, after their summer by the sea, there would be the return trip to Havana. Consuelo immediately started scheming for how she could manage to make the trip back with José by bus or train. She had a couple of months to think this through, and was sure that eventually she would come up with a believable story.

It was hot in Santiago de Cuba on the day they arrived, hotter than in Havana, and Consuelo started to wonder what Josefina had meant by the 'cooling sea'. She would give her this much: Oriente was beautiful, more beautiful to Consuelo than her own province. It had the tallest mountains she'd ever seen. They were covered in a dense canopy of jungle. A thick, green carpet started near the edge of town and reached upwards to cover the mountain, giving the city a spongy green backdrop. In front of them, the Caribbean Sea was a peaceful, undulating turquoise.

They'd arrived in Santiago de Cuba in mid- to late afternoon when most of the city was sleeping. Consuelo had yet to see much of the town, though they had driven through it slowly, Josefina pointing out the ice-cream parlor and the cinema, the Cespedes Park where they could take José, and a French restaurant Josefina particularly liked. They'd driven slowly up to the two-storied Spanish colonial dwelling facing the sea, Josefina referring to directions provided by the landlord in large, scrawling handwriting. When they found it Consuelo was truly excited. It was tall, powder blue, with Baroque detailing accented in white. The wrought-iron gate surrounding the house looked intricate, yet strong. The light blue contrasted well with the green foliage on the mountain and the sea, forming a continuum of blue to green broken only by the strip of gray road. For the first time Consuelo felt that she was somewhere really different, in a foreign land.

José was asleep, laid out in the back seat on some of the sheets and towels Consuelo had brought with them. She carefully lifted him and carried him up the front steps to the porch, which had a variety of white, Victorian wicker chairs, and even a porch swing. Josefina fished the keys out and opened the door, and they entered into a splendid, clean, cool mansion. The white and gray marble gleamed in the light coming in through the front door. Inside all the shutters were drawn and a couple of windows were opened slightly to let in the breeze. The house had retained the cool of the night before and now it welcomed them in.

Consuelo and Josefina went upstairs together and examined the bedrooms. They chose a large one with two beds for Consuelo and José, and the largest one, with a grand canopied bed, for Josefina. There were several more rooms besides, and Consuelo asked why Josefina had rented such a large house for just the three of them.

'I may want house guests.'

The sheets on the beds in her room smelled fresh and looked clean. She laid José down on one of them, gently kissing his head. She shut the door part of the way behind her, and then went with Josefina to explore the rest of the house.

The Baroque and Louis XV style furniture was tastefully arranged. The dining-room was large and grand, with a crystal chandelier, also in the Louis XV style. Around a large, walnut table, inlaid with ribbons of gold, was a set of Spanish Baroque style chairs, the leather looking worn and comfortable, the rivets gleaming. Imitation Picasso paintings were hung on two of the walls. One was a still life. The other was a very small reproduction of Guernica. You had to stand close up to it in order to see the detail. Consuelo had never seen a picture like it, and was disturbed by the bare light bulb and the disembodied cow's head. When Josefina wasn't looking, she crossed herself.

The kitchen was fit for an army of cooks and servants. Delaila would know what to do with all of this equipment, but Consuelo suspected that Josefina would be sorely disappointed

with the fare she would be dishing up for her. After explor-
ing the house, Consuelo brought in all the bags from the car,
dragging them up the steps to the second floor one step at a
time, resting halfway up to catch her breath. When she was
done her arms were weak and shaking. Next she examined
the contents of the kitchen: full English silverware and Ger-
man china sets, full cookware, but almost no food—a bag of
sugar, a bag of coffee, and some canned fish.

The cool of the evening was coming on, and Consuelo
decided she would need to go into town and get some food, for
the evening meal at least. José was now awake and downstairs
in the sitting-room with Josefina, staring at everything and
probably wondering how he'd arrived in this cavernous mansion, considering he'd fallen asleep in the back seat of a Ford.

'I'll drive you.'

Fear blossomed in Consuelo's heart, 'No … that's ok. I'll
walk. I want to walk into town. It's not far. It'll give me a
chance to look around.'

When she got back she cooked Josefina a simple meal of
an omelet naturel and an avocado salad. She carried the meal
into the dining-room on a lacquered tray she had found in
the kitchen. Josefina was seated at the far end of the table,
near the window. She was staring out into the darkness of the
trees and bushes in the back garden. José was on the rug
underfoot, playing with a toy caboose Rogelio had given him
a few days previously, an early birthday gift. Consuelo was
struck by the loneliness of this tableau.

Carefully balancing the tray on one arm, she put the serving platters, too large for omelet and avocado salad, in front
of Josefina. Consuelo stepped back, with the tray behind her,
and stood waiting for any requests from Josefina.

Josefina, not much of an eater, didn't mind the light supper. 'Get a plate and sit down with me.'

Consuelo stared at Josefina. She had never joined her at a meal before. She wasn't sure if Josefina was serious, and therefore didn't move. She awaited further instructions.

'Well? Why are you standing there? Have you had your supper?'

'No ...'

'That's a pretty big omelet—I see you've been taking lessons from Delaila on serving the masses. It's enough for two. You haven't eaten, so why don't you join me?'

Consuelo continued to stare at Josefina with apprehension. She wondered if this were a trick, and the minute she sat down, Josefina would become angry at her presumption.

'Stop staring like that, go to the kitchen, and get a plate and fork for yourself, woman!'

Consuelo responded to this more usual form of request, and turned for the kitchen. She fumbled for a set of cutlery for herself, a linen napkin like the one on Josefina's lap and a plate. She didn't take a china plate, however, but took one of the more common beige stoneware plates she found in a cupboard near the fire. She crossed the kitchen back to the door slowly, wondering if this were some sort of omen, wondering if it were bad luck to eat at the same table as your employer. She had to be honest with herself that she'd never heard of anything against it. She had no one to consult on this matter except a boy of three, and the woman who was inviting her to share this taboo pleasure. She thought for a moment more, shook her head, and went back out to the dining-room with her place setting.

When she reached the far end of the room where Josefina was sitting, she was surprised to note that Josefina had, very politely, waited for Consuelo to return before eating. Consuelo carefully laid her place setting by Josefina, picked José up off of the floor, and sat down in the chair with him on her lap.

'There, now, that's much better. Omelet?' To Consuelo's further surprise, Josefina carefully sliced and served some omelet and then some salad onto Consuelo's plate. Consuelo was fairly convinced at that point that if she were to look up into the night sky over Santiago de Cuba, she would see pigs flying.

José looked eagerly at the food, so Consuelo started cutting small pieces of the omelet and feeding them to José. While he was chewing, she took small bits for herself. She ate some of the avocado, and smiled to herself thinking, 'Well, it's only right that I should be subjected to my own cooking.'

'What was that smile for, what are you thinking?'

Consuelo told Josefina her private joke, and both women laughed. 'It's not bad at all! It's cooked well, and the avocado is ripe, and the lime and onion taste good. Enough vinegar, not too much, you did a good job.' Josefina underscored her comment by forking a load of avocado and onion into her mouth. Vinegar dripped down her chin.

After dinner, Consuelo cleaned up and put José to bed. She prepared a cafetera and brought this out to the front porch. She poured a cup for Josefina and one for herself, and sat down on one of the chairs near Josefina. Josefina was smoking a cigarette and offered one to Consuelo, who gladly accepted. Consuelo had a short but sharp pang of guilt, thinking of her stolen cigarette, but this faded quickly as she lit the cigarette and inhaled. They sat on the porch silently for a while, looking at the moon and the sea and the trees. There wasn't a sound but the breeze stirring the palm fronds. A ripe coconut was dislodged by the wind and fell, thumping on the road without breaking. Consuelo made a mental note to collect the coconut before she went to bed. There was no neighbor for many, many meters. It was quite unlike Havana.

Josefina and Consuelo started chatting. They discussed how well José was behaving on the trip. Josefina told Consuelo stories about Santiago de Cuba, and where some of the best linen could be purchased. They discussed Consuelo and her mother, and how energetic her mother was for such an old woman. Josefina asked about Miguel González, but Consuelo didn't have much to say, as she hadn't seen him in more than half a year. Their conversation lasted well past eleven bells, which they could faintly hear ringing out from the cathedral in the center of the city.

And from that night a relationship developed between Consuelo and Josefina that neither of them would have imagined possible only a few years previously. June in Santiago de Cuba brought them one pleasant evening after another. When Josefina was not visiting her brother's family, she would take her meals with Consuelo and José in the grand dining-room. José would be fed from both women's plates. Sometimes he would sit on Consuelo's lap and sometimes on Josefina's. Josefina's Havana friends were far away and in Santiago de Cuba they made their own little club of three.

They progressed from coffee together to wine, to Daiquiris that Josefina had to show Consuelo how to make. They would have one before dinner, then Consuelo, tipsy, would prepare a light meal, and after that they would have more wine over dinner, and then a coffee at the end. Sometimes, Consuelo left the dishes to be done until morning, too tired to be bothered otherwise. Josefina had no objection to this. Consuelo and Josefina would fall asleep together on the wicker chairs on the porch, their hair stirring lightly in the breeze, worn out from a day on the beach, minding José, drinking and eating.

José had turned three a couple of months earlier, and was

settling into his fourth year with aplomb. He was tall, thin and strong. He was well behaved and rarely disobeyed when indoors, but when outdoors lost the run of himself. Consuelo and Josefina spent sweaty afternoons chasing the boy around the park or the beach, trying to keep him from breaking a leg or an arm without discouraging his adventurous nature. He would climb into the woods behind the house, Consuelo chasing him into the canopy. She would run until she realized that she couldn't find him. The dappled sunlight coming through the canopy camouflaged José's movements. She would call his name until she saw movement, and then head for it, grabbing him and rolling him into her arms. He laughed and laughed and she put her face in his hair, tickling his neck with her lips.

Sometimes, in the afternoons after siesta, Josefina and Consuelo would take José into the city to Cespedes Park, and watch him play with other children who emerged from their apartments and mansions in the declining heat of the late afternoon. In these situations, Josefina had ample opportunity to start conversations with the other women in the park and leave Consuelo to mind her own child. This would have given her the chance to make new friends, more like her. But she didn't. She and Consuelo behaved like a unit with the sole purpose of caring for José and enjoying themselves together.

Though their shared interest was José, and therefore he was often the subject of their discussions ('I think he's grown a few centimeters'; 'He didn't eat his banana'; 'Isn't he clever? He assembled the little puzzle himself'; 'His vocabulary gets bigger every day'), he was not the sole topic. They also discussed the houses in Havana and Santa Clara and any changes that should be made to the décor or in their maintenance; how to best care for linen and silk; movies and movie stars' lives; Consuelo's hopeless brother; Josefina's idealistic brother; Rogelio's more amusing idiosyncrasies; the weather; the upkeep of the marina in Santiago de Cuba; Castro and the other rebels' progress in the East; Batista and the future of Cuba. Consuelo considered it to be the happiest month of her life.

He sashayed into the place looking thin, a bit ropey around the neck and arms, but healthy and bright eyed. He was wearing no tie, but a clean white shirt with a collar. He wore a black suit and a new leather belt with a silver buckle. Josefina choked a little on her Coca-Cola when she saw him.

She'd gone to the club that afternoon with José. Consuelo was happy to let them go off together so that she could have an afternoon to herself. She hadn't decided what she would do: take a walk, write a letter, examine the shops in the town, buy a half-dozen eggs and try her hand at flan. Her only worry was that Josefina would be taking José into town in the car. She consoled herself with the thought, 'The woman doesn't have that far to go in the car. What harm can she do? May Obatala protect them.'

Josefina and José had indeed made it in one piece to the club, and he was now playing tag in the lounge area with other children ranging in ages from three to ten. They ran in circles and made a racket that many of the mothers tried to hush, but that Josefina ignored or indeed encouraged. As José or another child was running past her, she would lean over and whisper loudly—'They're coming to get you!'— causing the child to squeal in fear and delight.

And this is how José ran into Rubén Castro's leg. José knocked himself to the floor, and his head bounced off the terrazzo. He cried bloody murder and wailed, 'Mamá!' in a tearful, plaintive voice. Josefina, still shocked to see Rubén, and now upset by José's knock on the head, rushed over and picked up the child. She kissed him and hugged him and felt his skull, but nothing seemed to be out of place. José's crying died down to a whimper and then nothing, and then he saw that the game among the children continued without him and he cried to be put down so that he could join them again. Josefina tried forcing him to rest for a few moments and sip a Coca-Cola. However, he could only manage this for several seconds before he was up and away chasing an eight-year-old girl.

Rubén had watched the goings-on with some interest. Now that José had left her, Josefina was sitting alone on a couch facing the sea. He looked around him. The club on a weekday afternoon was mostly women, who didn't recognize him with a shave, combed hair, and wearing a suit. Rubén approached Josefina and asked to sit next to her.

'You can do what you like. It's a free country.'

'More or less.' He smiled, and sat next to her. 'Lovely child, you're very lucky.'

'Yes.' Josefina smiled. She ordered a Daiquiri from a passing waiter. She felt a tingly sensation deep inside her, which she had not felt for years—since the last time she'd received a letter from Rubén.

'I'm sorry about knocking him to the floor like that, you must realize it was an accident.'

'Of course. Anyway, he ran into you. Don't worry about it, I think he'll live.'

'That's a good attitude. I hate mothers who are too over-protective of their children. Turns them into wimps.'

Josefina said nothing.

'Our mother, she let us roam free. We were climbing things, building little huts in the fields, breaking arms and everything, but I tell you, you learn quicker that way.'

'I'm sure. Speaking of, where is your brother?'

'Oh, he's around … You're looking very well.'

Josefina smiled unsteadily. Her Daiquiri arrived. Rubén finished his drink and asked for another from the waiter. They sat in silence for a couple of minutes until his whiskey arrived. Rubén dove into it with gusto, the ice hitting his upper lip, leaving droplets of the brown liquid on his mustache. He licked them off.

'I've missed you, Josefina.'

'Have you? That's hard to believe. I haven't heard from you in years. If someone misses a person, usually they make an attempt to communicate or even see them.'

'Well, communication hasn't always been possible. And I couldn't visit. I shouldn't even be here, really, but I needed a bit of a release after the last few weeks.' He stared at her intensely with a look that reached into her, straight down to the base of her spine, wrapping its hand around the cord and squeezing signals of desire to her brain.

Josefina took a deep breath and looked away for a moment to break the spell and compose herself. She looked back at him, 'Rubén—what are you doing out in public? I would assume the cops are after you … I mean, it's daylight—it's a Wednesday afternoon, for God's sake.'

Rubén chuckled, 'You're in the East now, Josefina. I have nothing to fear. Half the army and the cops are in our back pocket—haven't you seen the red-and-black armbands on some of them? Anyway, if anybody lays a hand on me here, all of these people,' Rubén swept a hand around the room, highlighting the waiters, the doorman, the pianist, 'All of them would rush to my aid. You're on my turf now, Josefina.'

'It's my turf, too. This is my town.'

'You left this town years ago.'

Josefina had no reply to this. She sipped at her drink. José ran over and stood in front of Josefina, staring at Rubén, 'Who are you?'

'A friend of your mother's.' Rubén reached out and patted José's check. 'You're a healthy-looking boy. Here, I may have something for you.' Rubén reached into his pocket and extracted a quarter. José took it from him, staring at George Washington's profile. He rubbed the shiny object in the palm of his hand and smiled.

'What do you say?' Josefina touched José's hand.

'Thank you, Señor.'

Josefina smiled approvingly, 'Now, take care of that. Put it in your pocket, and button it up.' José did so, smiled once more at Rubén, and ran off to join the children. Rubén called for another round of drinks. They sat in silence until the drinks arrived, staring at the water in the bay and the fort protecting its passage to the sea.

'So, Josefina, where is Rogelio?'

'In "the plain", where do you think? He rarely leaves Havana, and doesn't really come east. He thinks it's too wild. I'm doing "summer by the sea". He's doing summer in Lourdes Rodriguez's bed, I presume. Or maybe they are using ours this time … who cares anyway, I'm sure the maid will wash the sheets so I'll never know a thing when I return.'

'So things are pretty much status quo between yourself and Rogelio.'

'Status quo? They've deteriorated.' Josefina offered a cigarette to Rubén. He accepted it, and lit one for each of them. 'Listen, I may sound bitter, but things are actually better this way. I'm happier than I've been in years. We don't even bother pretending to ourselves anymore and that has taken all the stress away. To the world, we pretend, but I suspect we fool no one. It's fine the way it is, fine. We have occasional flare-ups of affection, but these brush fires are soon quenched. They serve to avoid a total blaze.'

Rubén reached out and put a hand on Josefina's knee.

She tried to suppress her laughter, 'You're funny.' She dragged on her cigarette, smiling around its edges, smoke escaping through the gaps between her teeth as if she were a smoldering volcano, letting off steam to avoid an eruption.

'No joke. I've always admired that knee … I've apologized for that night, Josefina, don't you believe me?'

'Yes, I do.'

'Do you accept it?'

'Maybe.' She eyed Rubén as he finished his second whiskey. 'But lay off the drink, will you? It's your Achilles' heel. It'll ruin you, it'll ruin this little revolt you have planned. And it'll ruin any chance you have with me.'

Rubén ordered a Coke. 'There's no fear any of what you say will come to pass, but I'm worried about ruining any feeling between the two of us.'

They sat in silence again, the sun declining behind them, the afternoon getting old, the edges of the boats on the bay blurring into the water, only their sails and masts distinguishing one from the other.

'Josefina, let's get out of here.'

She stood, stabbing out her cigarette in the ashtray stand, drinking down the last of her Daiquiri. She walked away from Rubén towards José, who lay on the floor near the bar. She pulled him up by his arm and walked him back over to Rubén. 'Let's go.' They slipped out of the club, down the darkened stairs and out to the Ford with none but the waiters taking any note.

Back at the house, Josefina entered first. She left Rubén in the sitting-room and went upstairs to put José down for a nap. Consuelo was neither in her room nor in any of the other rooms upstairs. Josefina went back down and told

Rubén that she would get them some soft drinks. She walked through the house to the kitchen. Still no sign of Consuelo. She opened two bottles of orange soda, and carried them back out to the sitting-room.

They finished their refreshments in silence, putting the bottles down on the coffee table when they were empty. Rubén didn't say a word, but approached Josefina like a leopard approaching an impala.

After a short, dreamy, fuzzy, hot end to the afternoon, Josefina lay awake in her bed, face to the wall, the sound of doves on the windowsill making her feel cozy, alive. Palm fronds brushed against the open shutters in greeting. Rubén remained asleep on the pillow next to her. She rose and washed her hands in the basin. She wiped a cloth under her arms and around her neck and breasts. She powdered herself and applied cologne. Rubén did not stir, no matter how much noise she made.

She sat at her dressing table, naked, watching him as he slept. He was on his side, facing away from her. The sheet moved up and down with the rhythm of his breath, with the expansion of his rib cage. It was folded down and only covered halfway up his torso. She could see his ribs poking at his skin. His arms, face and neck were a dark yellow-brown, the color of burnt paella. His chest, stomach and back were the color of vanilla pudding. He'd shaved only that morning, and he had a couple of nicks and scrapes on his neck. Josefina had touched these as they'd made love, wondering if he'd bled much, been wounded many times, in the preceding years. He broke the music of his sleep with a deep breath, almost a snore, then settled back again to quiet breathing.

Josefina had never touched a man other than Rogelio intimately. For years, she'd presumed that they were all pretty much the same. She didn't discuss details with anyone, but the women at her club often alluded, with sarcasm or dismay, to evenings when they were called on to do their wifely duties. Most enjoyed it. Some didn't. Some were indifferent.

Josefina wavered. Occasionally, she enjoyed it very much, and sometimes she just wasn't in the mood. In any case, she and Rogelio had fallen into a pattern, predictable as the summer rains. Then, they'd broken the pattern.

That afternoon she'd realized that if you made love to a different man, you actually did have a different experience. She thought, 'I'm an adulteress. This is what it's like.' She smiled. She liked the feeling. She felt she'd crossed over to the other side, raised herself up a level, and somehow liberated herself from her daily life. Rules applied to others, but not to her. She felt like a creator.

She wrapped herself in a silk robe, picked up a book, and lay back down next to him, reading by the fading light of day seeping through the lace curtains.

Josefina went downstairs in the evening when she heard activity in the rooms below. She slipped out of the room, and peeked over the railing at the balcony. She could see Consuelo's dark head moving about, tidying the sitting-room. She disappeared into the dining-room.

Josefina rushed down the hall to find José awake in his room, playing with a black yarn doll. She took him downstairs, put him on a dining-room chair, and told Consuelo that she would be resting in her room for the evening, and not to bother with dinner. Josefina made a large sandwich of leftover pork and Swiss cheese, poured a pitcher of milk, and brought them up to her room for Rubén.

At dawn, while Josefina and the others slept, Rubén slipped out of the house, to return to the mountains.

The following week, at around the same time Rubén Castro had first seen Josefina in the club, Consuelo heard a knock at the front door. She opened the double doors to the porch, and stood staring at Rubén. His face was somewhat obscured by the screen between them. Consuelo opened that, too, slowly, and continued to stare at him. Before she asked him what he was doing there, or did he want to come in, she wondered where his beard had gone, aloud.

'I just wanted to clean up for now. I'll grow it back. Don't worry, it grows fast, it'll be covering my face again within a week or two, and I'll be the man you've known all along.' Consuelo could not respond. She thought she was making Rubén uncomfortable, possibly for the first time in a long time. He was fidgeting from one foot to the other. He asked, 'Aren't you going to ask me in?'

Consuelo stood aside and Rubén entered the hall. She looked back outside and noticed two armed men on the porch, relaxing on the wicker chairs. She silently shut the door and pointed to the sitting-room. He walked ahead of her, and she followed him in and watched as he sat himself down comfortably on the settee, as if he was a welcome man in every household in the province. Consuelo furrowed her brows, experiencing a serious conflict between duty and desire.

'Is Josefina in?'

She thought for a moment. 'No.'

He took a cigarette case out of his jacket pocket. He offered one to Consuelo, who refused. He lit one for himself and returned the case to his pocket, staring at Consuelo as he did so. 'Will she be back soon?'

'Probably not.'

'I'll wait here.'

'Oh, will you?' Consuelo was rarely sarcastic or cutting,

but a fire had flared in her chest at hearing Rubén's presumption.

Rubén smoked, looking at Consuelo. 'You don't like that?'

'I'm not sure there's much I can do about it.'

'Why are you angry at me?'

'You just stopped writing. I haven't seen you in nearly five years. I mean,' she had a moment of remorse, 'I appreciated the money. But then that stopped, too. Where have you been?'

Rubén rolled his eyes, 'Another one … Listen—don't you read the papers? Where do you think I've been? I've been fighting for our liberation, I've been up to my knees in mud, eating nothing but rice—I've been fighting the fucking Batistanos, for God's sake, organizing the Precaristas, and I've been making progress, too. Why haven't you read about this?'

'They don't print all these stories, you know. Even I know that. Do you think they want us to know of all your successes?' Consuelo stood uncomfortably, staring at Rubén. Where to go from here? What to do with this man? He looked so small there, in front of her. With every passing year he had grown in her imagination, gotten taller and stouter and broader. And here he was now, stringy and thin: his strong, skinny neck poking out from his collar supporting a close-cropped head. He looked like a victim, not a perpetrator. And he looked like José. 'Oh, Rubén, of course I knew where you were. I knew when you fled the country, and I heard the rumors that you were back in '56 … I'm sorry, I'm just annoyed I didn't hear from you. Can I have one of your cigarettes?' He pulled out the case and handed her a cigarette, lighting it for her.

Consuelo sat next to him on the settee, smoking. 'You've

come to see Josefina? Not Rogelio? He isn't here, you know. How did you know she was here?' She looked at him questioningly.

'Rumors. They travel quickly and I know everyone in Santiago who spreads them.' Rubén paused here to accentuate his next utterance with a sincere glance, 'And I figured, where she was, you were.'

Consuelo's heart fluttered.

Rubén finished his cigarette, 'It's been a while, Consuelo, I know that, but that doesn't mean you haven't stayed in my mind. You've been a sharp image that hasn't faded, looking just as you do now—and you look good.' Rubén reached out to touch her face.

She pulled back, 'Please, Rubén. I won't believe that you care. I don't,' she stared at him defiantly to hide her lying.

'You should believe me, Consuelo. I care. If I didn't care for you, you lovely little thing, why would I have ever written at all? Why would I have sent Miguel to you?'

'This is true,' she thought. She said nothing.

Rubén put his hand on hers. He squeezed her fingers. 'I'm sorry you've been on your own for all this time.'

'I wouldn't say I've exactly been alone.'

Rubén ignored this, leaning into Consuelo's lips, brushing against them, then pressing against them. Conseulo didn't move. She was on an emotional fence, unable to either kiss back or pull away. Rubén squeezed her fingers again, and worked his hand up her arm, squeezing along the way: first at her forearm, then at her elbow, then at the flesh of her upper arm.

Josefina entered the room, holding José. Consuelo looked up, thinking, 'Not again.'

No one said anything for a moment. Josefina put José down, and told him to go up to his room and play with his toys until she came up for him in a while. He ran out of the room.

Josefina stood staring at her maid and her lover together on her rented settee. 'It's a topsy-turvy world, isn't it? When two-bit Leninists with nothing but old rifles and machetes can threaten the United States of America—and they watch powerless, almost disinterested, not knowing what to do?'

Neither Consuelo nor Rubén responded.

Josefina averted her gaze in disgust, 'Rubén—get out of my house.'

'Jose—'

For the first time in their lives, they heard Josefina yell, 'Get out! Now!'

He did. Consuelo stared after him, shame and hatred and love swelling at once in her breast, making her breathe heavily, making her think of her mother and Miguel and José and her brother and all that she'd left behind her, and wish that she had not agreed to spend this long hot summer with Josefina in a province where she knew not a soul … except for the one loved and hated revolutionary who'd just walked out. Consuelo got up from the settee. Josefina stared at her without speaking.

She paused on her way out and looked back at Josefina, deciding things must not be left so between them. 'Josefina, it's not what you think.'

'Oh, shut up, will you? You're like the worst kind of prostitute. Men don't even know what they're getting into when they accept your advances. Playing the sweet, the good, the virtuous young one. I see right through you. Rogelio, Rubén—who's next?'

'You've got it all wrong this time, Josefina.'

'Hardly. Listen—you are at my disposal. We leave early for Havana. We won't wait until the end of August. Another week to say our goodbyes and that's it. When we get back to Havana, Consuelo, you can organize your things and get the hell out of the house. I'm going to find a poxy old sow to do the washing. Now get out of my face.'

'I did not—'

'Consuelo, don't you see, I don't care what you did and what you did not—I just want you to go.'

Consuelo turned to leave the room, but Josefina called her name once more. 'And you can take the bus back yourself. José can go in the car with me. I wouldn't subject him to that sort of third-class treatment.'

'Don't bother, I will be the one subjecting him to it. He's coming with me.'

Unidos Debemos Estar

When she stopped talking, the quiet quickly became oppressive. The nurse had come and gone, checking blood pressure, heart rate, and listening to her lungs. Her diaper had been changed, though Josefina, when she could control herself, generally insisted on waiting until someone was present to walk her slowly to the bathroom. Lunch was an hour and a half behind us, and there was another three to go before dinner. When she didn't have visitors, Josefina filled these hours with the television or perhaps, if she had the energy, a crossword puzzle, using a magnifying glass to read the clues. She flipped through fashion or gossip magazines and occasionally read the paper, but was more often than not displeased by what she saw there, so she saved this activity for the weekend, when the *Herald* was filled with lighter pieces as well as serious ones. My stories were often in the weekend edition. Sometimes, she just sat staring in her room, perhaps recalling her past or, less likely, envisioning her future. It was quiet now between us, no sound of nurses in the hallway, no sound of birds from the tree just outside her window, the television off, the radio off. She shifted in her bed, waiting for me to make some response.

I looked back at her, this extinct volcano, this wrinkled peapod, past usefulness some would say—but not me. I was seized by love and pity. 'Abuela … that's … something else.'

'You don't look surprised.' She smiled, showing her gums, 'I was hoping for a bit of a shock. You know, it's hard to get my thrills these days.' She tried to look more serious, 'No, but really, I'm getting old. I don't want to take my stories to the grave. If I give them to you, I think they will maybe live on a little longer than I will. Or maybe I even think it's a way for me to live on myself, to defy time and nature.'

I weighed heavily in my mind whether this visit was the visit in which I shared the truth with her. I decided now was better than later, feeling a pang deep down inside that there would not be too many more 'laters' for Abuela Josefina. 'Abuela, I've heard this story before.'

She knitted her brows looking confused. 'How? I've told nobody. Does your father know this? Oscar?'

'No, Consuelo told me.'

'Consuelo? You've spoken with Consuelo? Where is she? How did you find her? What … did she say?'

'Sara and Rosa had a letter from her. She's told me lots of stories. She's helped me to fill in the holes. She's near Lakeland, in a house on a lake. Did you know this?'

'Yes. I knew this.'

'Did you know this for as long as she's been there?'

'Yes, I knew this.' Josefina looked upset and uncomfortable. She touched the drip in her hand, which kept her hydrated and which the nurse's aid used to give her medication twice a day. 'You liked her stories?'

'Yes—they were fascinating.'

'You like them better than mine?'

I smiled at Josefina, 'I like both the stories. I like her stories because they're about you and about her. I like your stories because they're about you and about her.' Abuela seemed only slightly mollified by this answer. 'I don't like her better, Abuela.'

Abuela tried to sit herself up in the bed. I jumped out of my chair to help her, 'Careful there.'

She looked annoyed, 'I can't believe I'm like this. I need a little flea to come and hoist me up whenever I want to change position.'

I kissed her cheek.

'Is Consuelo like this? In a nursing home like me, counting the hours until the end?'

'You're being a little over-dramatic there, Abuela, as usual. Last time I saw her she was not in a nursing home. She seemed sprightly, considering her age and all.'

'Hmph.'

'What have you got against her? You're mad that she kissed your boyfriend?'

Josefina looked angry, 'He wasn't my "boyfriend", don't be ridiculous. I was a married woman. We don't have "boyfriends".' She paused for a moment, 'He was my "lover".' She stared at me for about five seconds before we both broke out laughing. Josefina's laugh turned into a hack and cough. When she quieted down, she said, 'You wouldn't have a cigarette, would you?'

'You've got to be joking. You'll blow the oxygen tank. You know you're not supposed to. Anyway—I gave them up.'

'Good for you. Do you have any of your nicotine chewing gum?'

'That I've got.' I dug one out of my briefcase and handed it to her. She popped it into her mouth and started gumming it. 'Do you want me to get your teeth for you?'

'No—it's better this way—nothing to stick to. Also, my dentures pop out when I chew gum.' We started laughing again. Though age had ravaged Abuela Josefina in a thousand ways, it had definitely improved her sense of humor and sharpened her grip on reality. For some people, when they're at the bottom, the only way to look is up.

'Abuela Josefina, I love you.'

'I love you, too.'

I gave her a hug and sat back on a chair facing her bed, my back to the wall and the television set. Out the window, a cloud obscured the sun. Another followed and then another. Within a few minutes, the sky was a solid gray sheet. It threatened rain I knew it would deliver within the next hour then withdraw, leaving puddles on the streets and parking lots of South Florida gleaming in the evening sun. These puddles would probably not evaporate before tomorrow afternoon, when further showers would top them off. It was the rainy season.

'Abuela, Consuelo has told me a lot of stories. You've told me a lot of stories. Some have overlapped with each other, some have been unique to each of you. There's one that she's told me that I want to corroborate with you.' I thought for a moment, 'No, I don't want to corroborate it with you. I believe her. I mean ... I want to hear it from you. I want to know your point of view, because if there's one thing I've learned while working at the paper, it is that there are two sides to every story.'

T.S. Eliot's suggestion of how the world will end applies to the end of a certain Cuban world as well, to the end of Josefina's world. The cannon in the center of Havana sounded on 31 December, and all scurried to come inside as usual when they heard it. Last-minute curfews were a regular occurrence, an impotent weapon against the 800 rebels and their supporters—Oscar, Miguel and Rubén among them. Josefina and Delaila and Rogelio sat around the short-wave radio in one of the back bedrooms, listening to Radio Rebelde de la Sierra Maestra. Guevara and Cienfuegos had seized Santa Clara. Josefina clucked her disappointment, thinking about her farm. Rogelio assured Josefina that he had been in contact with the stewards and the groundskeeper, and the place was guarded and safe, for now.

Josefina and Rogelio were literally all dressed up with no place to go. They had planned to host a New Year's Eve party. Delaila had cooked enough party food to feed every rebel in the country, and it was waiting on trays carefully placed around the house. With the curfew on, no one would attend. Rogelio was annoyed, as all the food had been expensive, and now a lot of it would go to waste.

After a while the short wave faded to static and they turned it off. The three of them went into the sitting-room and ate bocaditos and cangrejitos and croquettas in silence. Around 11 pm the Machados and Margarita braved the local patrol, and ran quickly across the street to the Castillo house. At midnight, they popped open a bottle of champagne and sipped it in silence, the only other marker of the passage into 1959 being kisses on each other's cheeks, and the consumption of twelve grapes.

They finished four bottles of champagne between six of them—two of those present not being big drinkers—and Josefina woke on the morning of January 1st 1959 with a pounding headache and a sick feeling in her stomach. She dragged herself into the bath and lay there, unable to soothe herself back to sleep. She took two aspirin, got dressed and made up, and went into the sitting-room.

She smoked her cigarette standing by the window, seeing what she could of Havana. People were streaming onto the streets. She could see Margarita hug a waiter from the local café. Some of her neighbors came out cheering as well, waving scarves and handkerchiefs. 'So, it's true,' she said aloud in the empty sitting-room.

Delaila entered with a tray of coffee, 'Señora, I'm sorry to be so late with the coffee. I didn't think you'd be awake before noon.'

'Don't worry about it.' Josefina took the coffee from her and knocked it back in one shot. The heat of it singed her tongue. 'Delaila, I'll be going out. Please tell Rogelio when he wakes so that he doesn't worry. I'll be back later.' She put the cup back on the tray and left the room, collecting her handbag from the hallway.

Delaila hurried after her into the hall. 'Josefina—it's not safe. Batista's fled the country. The government has collapsed. There's no one in charge out there. It's madness.'

Josefina stared at Delaila for a moment, processing what she had said. 'I have to go out.'

Josefina tried to drive, but the crowds were too thick. She was within a few blocks of her destination when she had to abandon the Ford by the side of the road, locking it, hoping that this wouldn't be the last time she saw it. People thronged the streets. Someone grabbed her and kissed her fiercely on the lips—he looked deeply into her eyes and said, 'We are free!'

'I'm not.' She shoved him away from her, putting a screen of groups of people between herself and him. She clutched her bag to her chest, and pressed on into the barrio.

The road she was on was dusty and long. The houses were made of wood and tin and concrete. There were no ornate cornices here, no Baroque detailing, no American cars in carports at the side of the houses. Prostitutes were out in force, kissing and hugging their neighbors, passers-by, customers. Josefina shied away from them, pushing through the crowd, pushing towards her goal. She nearly tripped over a small dog she hadn't seen. He yelped and ran off, bumping into other people along the way. She could hear chickens, goats, children, the sound of large engines and celebratory gunfire. From a radio somebody had dragged out to their front porch, Josefina heard the now too familiar voice of Fidel on Radio Rebelde. 'This is a call for peace. This is a call for calm. I would like to tell the citizens of Cuba: please do not take the law into your own hands. We will be in Havana soon, and we will be dealing ourselves with any culprits and law breakers.'

She vaguely knew the way to the house, as she had been in the car when the driver had dropped Consuelo there several times before. After about thirty minutes she took her shoes off and put them under her arm, next to her clutch purse. The ground felt cool under her feet. As she walked she squeezed dust between her toes. She kept to the center of the road to avoid the gutter, pressing against the flow of revelers heading into the city. She stood out in the crowd: pale face and pale sweater in a sea of dark faces and lively patterns. Locals wore the colors of their patron orishas; yellow and green to the right of her, blue to the left, red and black together on a small man. Standing on a front porch next to a child, a goat with a handkerchief tied around its neck and painted horns watched her pass. A group of young men dressed all in white from head to toe—their dark faces stunningly beautiful, an even creamy chocolate above crisp linen and cotton guayaveras—clapped in rhythmic unison as they walked in towards Old Havana. Dark women wore red lipstick, making their lips look purple, contrasting with the skin of their chest. Josefina was swimming against the tide in a sea of beautiful, tropical fish.

She arrived at the small house, a shack she thought, about an hour and a half after she'd abandoned the car. The crowds were thinner back here. The gate was latched closed but the doorway was open, and in it stood José, almost an inch taller than when she'd last seen him, holding a piece of bread in one hand and a stick in the other. He ate greedily, staring at Josefina. He was wearing the last pair of trousers she'd bought for him, which were now shin-length. His shirt was also too small, the sleeves stopping somewhere along his forearm, the buttons at the sleeve and down the front left open so that he would have freedom of movement. He was neat and clean, but he had a hungry, vacant look in his eyes. A skinny black dog stood panting, staring up at José, hoping for a crumb. Josefina smiled at him from the gate, fluttering her fingers in greeting.

'Who are you?'

Josefina flinched. Did children have such short memories? 'It's your—it's me, Josefina. Don't you remember me and my house and all the things we did?'

José smiled, stepping forward, still looking at her with some confusion. 'Your hair is blonde. Josefina has the brown hair.'

'I just put some color in it for fun. The brown will grow in soon. Or I can go to the salon and change it tomorrow.'

'I think you should do that.'

'Maybe I will—just for you. Is your mother home?'

'Mamá!' José turned and ran back into the house. Josefina

stood nervously by the gate, waiting.

Consuelo took her time before eventually emerging into the daylight, squinting. She observed Josefina in silence from the single front step for a long minute. After much deliberation she went over and opened the gate and, still in silence, walked back into the house, followed by an unsure Josefina.

Once inside, Josefina stood near the crucifix, Christ's loincloth clean and white, but all paint faded from his hands and torso.

Consuelo decided she would initiate their verbal waltz, in the hope of ending the meeting as quickly as possible, 'I have nothing to offer you but water.'

'No, thank you.'

'I could mix it with soil from the yard for you, if you're so inclined. It makes a muddy porridge, but if you stare at it long enough you can imagine it's chocolate or perhaps badly burned cream of wheat.'

They said nothing more between them for a while as they stared at each other angrily.

Josefina looked away and out the door to the brutal blue sky. 'I have money for you.'

'Rubén has promised to send me to the East to help with the Revolution. Today is not the end; it's the beginning. I don't want your money.'

'Consuelo … When did you make José? Was it in my bed, with Rogelio?'

'Santa Clara. July of '53.'

Delaila had sent Consuelo into town to pick up some items she'd needed for the evening dinner. Josefina was out riding with women from the neighboring estate and Rogelio dropped Consuelo into the town center in the morning. He was going to the far side of the province with the overseer in order to purchase some new equipment for the farm. Consuelo had told him that she would take the bus back to their estate—she would probably be done with her shopping earlier than Rogelio could collect her. It would be more convenient for her to bring home the purchases that way. He agreed to pick her up at the end of the road near the farm in the late afternoon, where the bus stopped to drop off passengers on its way to Cienfuegos.

Consuelo enjoyed her afternoons in Santa Clara. She could be alone, and look in the shop windows and see different people walking about on their errands. It was a central, provincial capital, in no way comparable to Havana or Santiago de Cuba, but she liked it for this. She liked it for its lack of pretension, for its isolation, for the pungent smell of oxen and fruit that wafted across from fields into the town center and whispered to all the city dwellers: you are of this country, this land made you.

Consuelo stopped at a coffee shop for the rare treat of 'eating out'. She put her empty bags, to be filled with goods later, at her feet. She ordered a café con leche and a pastellito de guayava. The fruit pastry was placed in front of her along with the steaming cup of milky coffee. She sipped at it, blowing at the hot froth to cool the mixture. There were not many in the café during mid-morning. Cafés were busy early, before the workday, and again at lunch. There was a lull at mid-morning, and a long, unattended afternoon stretch after lunch when no work was done, no patron was served, until the sun went down. Occasionally, for very desperate customers, a beer would be popped open and poured over ice in a tall glass.

A small group of men appeared as Consuelo was finishing the pastry. They looked serious yet joyous, intent. They dressed like anyone else, but after a few moments, she thought to herself: 'Those are rebels.' She recognized two of them: Rubén and Fidel. She had served them drinks before, years before, at a party hosted by the Castillos.

The man behind the counter greeted the men with a wave and a smile—this was a sympathetic town; or at least a sympathetic establishment that she was in. They took their hats off and wiped their brows. The men ordered juices and Coca-Colas. Some ordered beers. Rubén Castro gave them an angry look—he obviously wanted them to stay sober. He ordered water and papaya juice.

Consuelo knew Fidel was known as the man in charge but, though he wasn't better looking than Fidel, she couldn't take her eyes off of Rubén. He deferred to his brother constantly—lighting his cigars, bringing him his drink, pouring water for him from a jug on the counter. Fidel had the charisma, but she thought Rubén had the silent smarts of the organization. When he spoke, people listened to him. She listened to him.

The men made themselves comfortable around a table. Someone pulled out a set of dominoes from a bag. They put them face down and started to mix them around, the tiles making clinking noises against each other and on the wooden tabletops. Each took a few and turned them over so that they could see their draw, shielding their selections from their neighbors. They started to put them down, creating a geometric Aztec pattern on the tabletop.

Rubén was not playing. He was looking at Consuelo, alone at her table, wearing a cotton dress and sandals, not her uniform. She had powdered her face that morning against the heat, and dabbed violet water on her neck. She'd applied a light rose shade to her lips, which she had found on Josefina's dresser when she was making the beds. Rubén recognized her. He gave her a half smile and held up one hand in greeting. Consuelo returned in kind. A waitress asked her if she wanted anything else. Consuelo said no, thank you. She had already paid for her snack. She looked back to Rubén.

He was approaching now, smiling as he did so. He grabbed a chair and scraped it across the concrete over to her table. 'May I?'

'Of course.'

'Nice to meet you again. I remember you from the Castillos' house. You're still with them?'

'Yes. They have a farm here. We're here for a couple of months. There's a harvest.'

'Oh, yes. I forgot Josefina had the farm this way.'

'Have you spoken to her lately? I know you saw her at that dance recently.'

Rubén took his time and lit a pipe, considering his answer. 'Yes. We talked a little bit. But then she went to another club and I had friends to meet.'

Consuelo nodded. She understood that someone like him would be a very busy man, know a lot of people, have a lot of commitments, that he wouldn't always be able to talk to people. She was pleased that he was taking a moment to talk to her. They spent another hour or so talking about Santa Clara as opposed to Havana; the beauty of Oriente Province where he was from; the Castillos' rich friends; Consuelo's family; the music she liked; the people she knew; her mother; her dog.

It was lunchtime in Santa Clara. Consuelo still had not done any of her shopping. She picked up her bags and explained to Rubén that she would have to move on.

'Why not have lunch with us?'

She didn't have enough money for a meal, but tried to find another excuse to decline. Rubén cleverly explained, 'We get free lunches from this establishment anyway.'

Consuelo joined them at the table. She sat between Rubén and Fidel. Fidel ate slowly. People waited for him to start before they lifted their forks. The others ate heartily. They devoured everything, greedily stuffing bread and pork into their mouths, followed by gulps of mango juice, cream soda, water, milk or beer. She picked at her tasajo, confused by the conversations, unsure of the definition of the words they were using. At the beginning of the meal, she had had no idea of what their cause was, of what they were fighting for, why people loved them or hated them, supported them or wanted them jailed. By the end, she couldn't understand why anyone would stand in their way.

After coffees, Rubén followed Consuelo outside. They lit cigarettes and stood looking up and down the street. The sun shone down uninterrupted in its path from the center of the solar system to the center of Cuba. It baked the streets from the cloudless sky. The town was quiet. Shutters were drawn, curtains pulled closed, lunches finished, everyone in bed. A lone bicyclist made his way down the main street, ice-cream trolley in tow. 'Granizados ...' he called to an absent public.

'Oh dear, the shops are closed. I've had a great morning, but now I'm going to have to wait it out until they open. I'll be late for the bus.'

'I'll drive you back.'

'Thanks, but I still have to wait for the shops to open.'

'Let's go to the park. We can sit in the shade of a tree. It's too warm in the café.'

They walked quietly down the street to the park. They entered a neat, colonial square framed by Flamboyan trees and Royal Palms. They found a bench under a tree in a corner and sat down. Neither smoked. They didn't speak. Consuelo found it no cooler in the shade, as she felt that Rubén was generating vast quantities of heat, which were enveloping her, intoxicating her. She stared at the bandstand in the center of the park. Rubén reached out and took Consuelo's hand. He pressed it to his lips. She didn't shrink away or remove her hand from his grasp. He kissed her wrist. He kissed her forearm. She didn't move. He kissed her elbow. She giggled and pulled away in reflex, unable to suppress a laugh. 'I'm very ticklish there.' He laughed too.

They spent a while in silence, Rubén kissing her hands, her fingernails, her wrists, her face, her neck, looking at her with his big, round eyes.

'Don't you need to nap? If you're going to Santiago de Cuba later today, that's a long journey—you'll need your energy. It's hot.'

Rubén smiled, 'Let's take a nap.' They got up from the bench, and Rubén led the way to an inn run by friends of his, the Acostas.

The door opened into cave-like darkness. They entered, rubbing their eyes, trying to adjust their vision to the dimness inside. The hostess of the inn smiled, welcoming them. The two of them made their way upstairs. Rubén paid for nothing.

The room was clean and large with high ceilings. The shutters were halfway open, keeping in some of the cool, letting in some of the sun. There was a wicker chair near the floor-to-ceiling window and blue voile curtains. There was a wooden dresser, painted green: the room was as she remembered it. She'd been there many times before with different men. The overseer, some of the peasants who worked the gardens around the house, the man in the café where she'd had her mid-morning snack—they all used the same inn. It didn't cost much, and it was well kept, clean and attractive, and centrally located. The owners were discreet bohemians who believed in free love and everyone's right to it.

Consuelo had thought she'd loved them all and they her. She couldn't help herself. She was seized by the beauty in each man particular to him. They all had something interesting about them: one a face; another a sense of humor; another, mystery. She always saw possibilities in them, a future. She was somewhat picky. It couldn't just be any man. It had to be one that shone from within. And it could never be her employer. Soon after each encounter she'd discover that they were often not as interested in her unique quirks as she was in theirs. Sometimes, they were. She never regretted any encounter.

She didn't point any of this out to Rubén. This was a new man, and thus a new experience, never done before, never felt before. They lay down and made love during the heat of siesta. Afterwards, they fell into a dozy, uncomfortable sleep. They weren't there for long before Consuelo said she had to go run her errands, and Rubén said he had to meet the others for their trip east. She felt affection for him. She wanted to see him again. He didn't know if that was possible—they had big plans for the coming months and he didn't want to endanger her by getting her involved. Would he visit her in Havana? Rubén said he'd see what he could do. Hopefully, he would be back to Havana soon, and they could get an ice cream together. They walked into a dull, cloudy, late afternoon, Rubén going back to the café and Consuelo turning up another lane to go and make her purchases.

She did her shopping and in the end did miss the bus. She didn't see the rebels or their cars in front of the café. She headed for the road home on foot. She was walking with the heavy bags when she was passed by two large Oldsmobile cars carrying the rebels. One car stopped and offered her a lift. She rode the rest of the way back to the Castillo farm sitting next to Fidel Castro. He was twice her size and took up over half the seat. He was clean shaven, with the most beautiful profile she'd ever seen. Rubén was in the other car. She turned to look out the window in the back, but couldn't see him. She got out of the car at the gates to the farm and waved the rebels off as they drove away, wishing them good luck.

'I didn't see him again until he came by the house in Santiago. And then, I only saw him for a short while.' Consuelo was sipping water, standing at the door to the kitchen.

Josefina was on the sofa, staring at her. A long silence inhabited the space between them for five minutes or more. Finally, Josefina spoke, 'When are you going east?'

'I don't know. Maybe I'll wait to be called. Maybe I'll head out and find a lift tomorrow from others heading to meet them in Santa Clara, for the march west into Havana.' Josefina had nothing to say to this. Consuelo filled the void, 'I should have joined them in the mountains years ago, Josefina, and not wasted my time in your house. I should have gone to Mexico. I should have worked with Miguel in the underground. I would have, but for ...' she trailed off.

'Why won't you take money then? José ...' Josefina stopped and changed tack, 'Have you eaten?'

'Why did you come here? To throw me a few pesos and then head off? You can't fool me that you feel compassion, because I've seen the depths of your compassion, Josefina, and I can put my finger into that fount and it wouldn't get wet. If you felt compassion, you wouldn't have sent me away. You would have been here months ago. You wouldn't have left me to raise this child with my mother in the cemetery, an unemployed idiot for a brother, and a dead goat as our sole livestock.' José watched from the doorway. Consuelo looked up at him, 'Go next door to Yamile. Tell her I have to go out for a short time I'll be back soon. Don't ask her for milk;

remember your manners. Just sit quietly on the sofa, or play with their boy.' José ran off.

When he was gone, Josefina continued. 'I didn't know any of that. How could I know these things?' Her trademark ire flared up, 'For God's sake, woman, because I yell once, get angry once, you think our world has ended. Don't you know me yet? Your strategy should have been: wait for me to cool down … and then come back. Ask again. Does history not teach you?'

'Me ask you, me go back to you, after being dismissed twice? Please, even I have pride. Just tell me what you want, already … Don't like Margarita's mending? Can't find another wretched servant? Amongst all the starving guajiros in this country, no one else can wash your clothes?' Consuelo felt a release she had never felt before and told me that she would not feel again in her life. She felt herself empowered, moving up a level, growing an inch, gaining weight and stature like a threatened animal fluffing its coat, spreading its wings, or baring its fangs. Her dam was breached, and sewer water poured out. Josefina made no immediate answer, and Consuelo took the opportunity to continue, 'Would you rather, if anyone is going to seduce Rogelio, that I seduce Rogelio? Is that it? He makes me sick, by the way. Bile rises up in me when he enters the room and it's all I can do not to pour a scalding pot of chicken broth over his head and stuff buttered bread into his briefcase. So if you are sick of sleeping with him, you'll have to find another domestic to do it because I won't. Perhaps Delaila would oblige? She's never once said no to you. You could give it a try.'

'I want José.'

Consuelo rubbed her face with her hands and sat on the couch. The springs gave a squeak. She started giggling a bit. It turned into a laugh. She bent over and laughed into her hands, her shoulders shaking and her fingers digging into her hairline, leaving fingernail half moons on her forehead.

Josefina stood staring at her, unsure what to do and how to proceed. She'd gone there with no plan, but with an expectation that her request wouldn't be received badly. She could not tell if the laughing were good or bad.

Consuelo's laughing subsided. She leaned back on the sofa, her hands falling from her face into her lap, her expression slackening, her eyes gazing above her to Christ on the cross, and then out to the soil in the yard, and the road beyond it leading east. She thought of the starving boy she'd sent next door. She imagined the end of one life and the beginning of another, the turquoise Caribbean, the undulation of white scarves on a clothesline. She looked back to Josefina.

Josefina stood silently in her bare feet, watching Consuelo carefully. She held her shoes and purse firmly under one arm, the other wrapped around her waist.

'I love you, Consuelo. And I love that boy. I'd save you both, but I'm willing to take one. Give me the boy. He'll have the best of everything. He'll have our accent. I'll send him to Belén, then to university. I'll feed him too much and he'll grow fat and happy like my brother. He won't cut cane and he won't clean toilets. You can come and see him anytime. But don't take him to the fields, don't take him to the mountains. He's too young to work, and too young to understand your Revolution.'

'It's our Revolution. The world is changing. It's not the same, Josefina. Why do you think I'll give him less than you can in the future?'

Josefina kneeled before Consuelo, drawing eye-level with her. 'When you are in that position, come and get him from me. I'm just a port for him to dock in.'

That evening, Rogelio found José asleep in one of the guest bedrooms. He went to look for Josefina. She was in the laundry-room, sorting through José's clothing, determining what would still fit and what she should keep, and what to give to poor children in Consuelo's neighborhood. She looked up to see Rogelio standing in the doorway, giving her a quizzical look.

'Is Consuelo here? Is she working here?'

'No.' Josefina put the clothing down to repeat the line she had rehearsed in her head for hours, 'She has run off to join the Revolution. José is ours now.' Rogelio's only response was to stand in the doorway, looking astounded. Josefina continued, 'He's our baby boy. You've always wanted a son ...'

'I wanted my own son, not somebody else's black baby.'

'He's not black—he'll pass. He's fair enough. His hair's not curly. Anyway, who cares? You love that child, you know you do.'

'Ave María, Josefina, you can't get pregnant, so your solution is to take someone else's baby?'

She didn't have any hate left in her to react to Rogelio's fire with fire. 'I didn't take him. Rogelio, listen to me, she's run off. She's on a bus or in the back of a pick-up truck heading east right now as we speak. Tomorrow she'll be learning to fire a gun or use a hoe—I don't know what.'

Rogelio shook his head, leaning against the doorframe. He repeated the unbelievable, 'She's gone off ... without him. The child ...'

'Yes. He's ours now to take care of. She may come back, I don't know, but he's ours ... essentially ours.'

Rogelio gave in as easily to this desire as he did to any of Josefina's other requests and demands. If nothing else, he had a highly developed sense of guilt about his infidelities and the fact that he just didn't love her. He lit a cigarette, 'I suppose a black baby is better than no baby at all.'

'Consuelo never did see him again.'

The afternoon rains had passed and I'd wheeled Abuela Josefina outside. I was sitting next to her on a low concrete wall in the entrance to the nursing home. Our view was the parking lot. Neat rows of SUVs and pick-up trucks obscured our view of the passing traffic, but we could hear them buzzing by and could just about smell exhaust fumes. Across the street was a strip-mall. I chewed furiously on my Nicorette gum, using every shred of willpower I possessed not to run across the street and buy a pack of Marlboros.

Josefina closed her eyes and tilted her face up to the sun, smiling faintly.

'Do you want me to put some sunblock on you, Abuela? You'll get a burn.'

'No, no. I like this sensation. I'm getting sick of that air conditioning in there. I want the feel of the burn to remind me that I've been outside. That I actually have skin. There was no air conditioning when I was a child, you know. Or even when I was older. We just had ceiling fans or hand-held fans. And we took naps in the day to avoid the worst of the heat. It worked. It was a nice life. I miss it, most of it. Well, some of it.'

We sat quietly for a while. I spit out my spent nicotine gum and put another in my mouth. 'This boy … where is he now?'

Josefina looked at me quizzically.

'Consuelo has told me this story. She told me she thought he would be better off with you. She was working in the East, and within a few years you'd fled to Miami with Rogelio and the boy and you didn't tell her. But what I haven't been told is where the boy is now.'

She furrowed her brow, 'I thought Consuelo had finished the job for me.' Josefina reached out one shaky hand and touched my fingers, 'My dear, José is your father.'

It felt like a small grenade had exploded in my belly, sending its rainbow shrapnel upwards into my brain. My mind was temporarily filled with these colors and all thought and feeling was obliterated. Was this Joyce's epiphany, or just a kind of shock? 'But ... Dad's name is Juan.'

'We bribed someone to issue a false birth certificate.' Josefina stared at me, hopeful.

The light and color were seeping down and away from my mind, my field of vision was clearing, less blue. I looked at Josefina more closely: thin, brown hair; feline green eyes; sharp bend of nose. How could I ever have thought otherwise? 'We're not related? And you waited almost twenty-five years to tell me this—all of you? No one could just tell me?'

'Marysol, I'm as related to you as Consuelo is. We share no blood, but trust me I'm deep inside of you. I'll always be. Juan is my child. He was always my child, even before he was born. He loves me like his mother, and Rogelio like a father. Rogelio was always wonderful with him—everything he was not with me. Juan has almost no memory of Consuelo.'

'Almost.'

Josefina said nothing.

'Is that why he hung up on me last year when I went to visit her? I called him on the phone to tell him I was visiting this woman who seemed to be a major part of your past, and he got angry and hung up on me. He told me that he was annoyed that I'd gone off without telling them where I was going, and that they were worried about me. But he just wants to write her off entirely, is what you're saying.'

'Maybe so. Please understand, I don't talk to your father about it and he doesn't talk to me about it. It's been this way for years, forever in fact. We see no reason to change now. His strategy is not to remember, to block out Cuba and move forward. Mine is to remember again and again. To replay my life, to you, to friends, and to see if there is something I can learn when I repeat the story again, when I think through the events one more time.'

'This is ... unreal.'

Josefina laughed. 'Life is unreal. It's what you choose to believe and hold onto that's real.'

Recordando A Aquellos Que Muertos Están

I was hoping for a funeral like the ones you see on television. Hundreds of mourners in black to pay their respects, a steady pouring rain from heaven to mark the occasion, the streets deserted, a large reception afterwards where everyone drank and shared stories, like an Irish wake. In fact, it was a stunningly sunny day. There were few at the funeral parlor the night before: Sara and Rosa, Isabelle and Oscar, my mother and father, our old neighbors Marielena and Gladice. Gabriella had passed away years ago, and Maria could not be reached. There was an open casket, in front of which I stumbled. I reached into the coffin and grabbed at the rosary clasped against her chest in her cold hands. Sara and Rosa pulled me off and helped me to sit in one of the folding chairs. We sat in silence for the rest of the evening, staring at the coffin and occasionally praying.

The next day I shed not one tear as they lowered the coffin into the ground, next to Rogelio's grave. The priest said his words and we made the long walk among the palm trees and rose bushes back to the cars in gray silence. My heels sunk into the earth as I walked—I'd worn an old pair of Josefina's in tribute, though I was inexperienced at walking in them. They were half a size too big and kept slipping off my heel, leaving a red mark.

As I approached the cars I saw a small, round figure under a tree near the gates. It hovered like the angel of death, watchful and unforgiving. She was dressed in black and observed our group as we got into the cars. I would recognize Consuelo even if I were blindfolded. No one else projected such a straightforward, musky presence. We looked in each other's direction. She was far away and I couldn't tell if her eyes actually met mine. She was holding flowers. I got into the car without greeting her or pointing her out to anyone in the group.

It was during the evening reception at Oscar and Isabella's house that Sara passed me a phone message Rosa had picked up from the answering machine. Consuelo was at a Motel 6 on the Tamiami Trail, a busy, low-rent artery that cut Miami in two. She'd left a number. She would be driving back up to Lakeland the following day.

Phoning her seemed like betrayal, but not calling seemed so as well. I rubbed the paper between my fingers, looking at the information in Rosa's neat writing, and then stuffed it into my handbag, which I left in one of the bedrooms. I rejoined the small family gathering in the living-room and poured myself a glass of water. I sat as in Shiva the rest of the afternoon, distracted, not hearing others' words, not eating, not speaking, not reading or watching the television. I left with my parents around seven and went to sleep in my childhood bed around nine o'clock that night, clutching

Consuelo's phone message between my fingers.

I didn't get out of bed until nearly eleven the following morning. I hadn't been sleeping, I'd just been laying there, thinking of nothing in particular, thinking about when I should go back to work, thinking about the new education and science correspondent they'd hired at the paper (he was good looking, Argentinean), thinking about Josefina and what she would think of him, and thinking about Papí.

I pulled a T-shirt on over my pajama bottoms and went into the kitchen. There was food in bowls and trays and boxes all over the place. Isabella had forced Mamá to bring home cold cuts, bread, pimento sandwiches, fruit and cakes. I lifted the foil off of a sandwich tray and poked my finger into a small pimento sandwich, a bocadito, to test its freshness. It was stale but I ate it anyway, washing it down with a Diet Materva I found in the fridge. This opened up my appetite, and I set about ransacking the trays for the freshest bits. When I was done I pined for a cigarette, but tried to push this to the back of my mind with thoughts of a strong coffee. I put the large cafetera on to boil—surely someone else would need coffee soon—and looked out the window.

Papí was out back in a lawn chair, staring at the avocado tree. He wasn't smoking or drinking coffee, he was just sitting alone, the *Miami Herald*, unopened, held loosely in one hand. Mamá was back at work. Isabella and Oscar would probably be by soon to visit us as they had promised. When the cafetera steamed and bubbled over, I prepared two tiny cups of Cuban coffee and went to join my father outside. I handed him his coffee, which he accepted silently, and pulled a rickety lawn chair next to him. I sat down, my bare feet digging into the dewy grass, and sipped on my coffee.

The Russell avocado tree out back was beautiful. I could see why he was staring at it. It had been there for many years, and had come with the house. The variety had originated in the West Indies and brought to Florida in the early twentieth century. The tree was thick and strong, maybe two feet around and forty or fifty feet tall. I loved the laurel-shaped leaves and dark bark. Mamá sometimes let neighborhood kids play in the tree and in the big back . I noticed that some-one had carved their initials into the bark near the bottom. Probably a child. At first I was annoyed, and then I thought, 'Posterity. The tree will survive the graffito and possibly out-live the child.'

The tree produced its buttery fruit like clockwork every August and September. They had just ripened recently, but the long, gourd-like avocados had been left rotting on the ground over the last couple of months, everyone too preoc-cupied with Josefina to bother gathering them. And the grass was tall out back, almost too tall to see them. They would ruin the mower.

'Haven't cut the grass in a while, Pops.'

'No …' he sipped on his coffee.

I wanted to engage my father in conversations like the ones I'd had with Abuela Josefina and Consuelo, but I didn't know where to begin. I'm not sure what made my conversa-tion with him any different than my conversations with any-one else. Maybe it was because I had to initiate them. Maybe it was because the conversations were practical, mechanical and respectable. They didn't let me in to any emotional land-scapes; they didn't reveal anything that shouldn't be revealed. This is possibly a good quality in a disciplinarian father, but a bad quality if you want to develop emotional intimacy with someone. I was ashamed to admit to myself that I just wasn't interested in what he had to say most of the time. But I thought it was important that I made myself interested. Jose-fina and Consuelo had made me realize that my dad did indeed have a history, like we all had a history. He had a story: but how to extract it?

And I thought, 'If you're going to start, just start.'

'I suppose you're missing her?'

'No, actually, not at the moment. Right now I'm thinking, "This tree needs a pruning."' We laughed a little, neither of us letting our laughter be too loud or last too long out of respect for our role as mourners. I let the last comment lie for a while, thinking of other questions I had for him.

'Dad, what do you think of Castro?'

'Castro? What, are you doing a report for work?'

'No—no, I'm just curious. I never hear your political views. I mean, I know generally … but, anyway, what do you think?'

'Em … probably like what most people think: he's a dictator, he's too old, he's been in power for a ridiculous amount of time, he should hold free elections, he should not take political prisoners; planned economies sound nice but are impossible to implement—does that about cover it?'

'I guess so. When he dies, do you think there will be elections, or do you think Rubén Castro will just take over?' I looked at my father's face very carefully, noticing every crease, the position of the corners of his mouth, looking for anything that might betray emotion.

His features did not change, not even a quiver. 'I don't know. Maybe there'll be elections, I hope.'

I could see that that wasn't the right approach. I tried to think of a better one … and then I realized I didn't need an approach. The best way to deal with my father was to just come out and ask. 'Ok, Dad, listen … I know. Ok? I know that Abuela Josefina is not technically my Abuela. I know that there is another woman who is your mother. Her name is—'

'Please, Marysol!' My father raised his voice. I was shocked into silence. This was a rare occurrence. 'Please ... I don't want to know her name.'

'You don't remember her name?'

'Of course not—I just remember calling a different woman "Mamá" for a while. It's a very vague memory. More like a dream I had. I like it that way. Fuzzy. Maybe it never really happened. It's unimportant what her name was—'

'What her name is.'

'It doesn't matter.' He looked away from the avocado tree for the first time, 'My mother is dead. Drop it. I'm glad you know. In case we get any genetic diseases we know where to go.'

This shut me up. I finished my coffee and put the cup on the grass. Papí did the same. We went back to staring at the avocado tree but this didn't last long. I had to press on, I had to know, I had to have a history like everyone else, my history, 'Dad ...'

'Yes, Marysol.'

'Dad—you are, like, part of the Revolution. It's in your blood.'

My dad half chuckled and half sighed, 'I suppose tenacity is why you have the job you do and do it well, eh? Marysol—I don't believe that "in your blood" garbage. Ok? We make our own futures; we have our own interests. Just because you and I are related to Rubén Castro does not mean we are going to take up arms and overthrow the mayor of Coral Gables. Just because I have a biological mother somewhere else does not mean that I am any less Josefina—or that you are any less Josefina. More if anything else. You have the same sharp intellect: questioning, not fully trusting, tenacious, insightful ... concentrate on these facts.'

'But Papí—I'm this other woman, too. Open, earthy.'

'Listen,' Papí got up from his chair, folding it, picking up his coffee cup from the grass, 'that's for you. I don't want to know. It's not for me. The information is just not for me. Move on.' He put his lawn chair back against the side of the house, under the overhang that kept them dry, and walked up the steps and back into the kitchen, leaving me out back to stare at the avocado tree on my own.

Hacia Un Ideal

Itook the same road I'd taken the year before, but this time I was driving my parent's car, a newer, sturdier SUV. I didn't feel the heat on my neck this time, no patches of cool or hot to signal movement through a stand of trees or a sunny field. The place held no mystery now, but instead tension. The lines in the road were drawn taut, the houses set on the edge of their plots. The numbers on the houses were climbing with meaning, culminating in Consuelo's. The house looked the same. It had not been repainted in the intervening year. The lawn looked a little overgrown. The plants a bit weedy. There was a different car in the driveway that I pulled in behind.

I knocked on the door, worry a knot in my stomach, the heat contrasting with the cool of the air-conditioned car and making me a bit dizzy. The door opened and an unfamiliar, middle-aged blonde woman stood looking at me.

'Hello. Can I help you?' She had a Southern accent and

was smiling widely in response to my furrowed brows and confused look.

'Is Consuelo here?'

Her look turned to one of worry, 'Oh, dear, I'm sorry to inform you, she's in the hospital. She's not feeling well. I'm taking care of the animals for her while she's away, and I decided to clean the house for her as a surprise.' I looked behind her and noticed a mop and a bucket. There was no fruit in front of the Virgin on the shelf, and the smells of food, incense and animals had been replaced by those of artificial pine and bleach.

'Hospital …?'

'The Lakeland Regional Medical Center … it's not too far. I can draw you a map or point it out for you if you have a map.' I stood looking at her without speaking, rather rudely, I thought. She kept a smile on her face, though, 'Are you a relative?'

I thought for a moment, 'Yes, I am.'

'Well, I hope she gets better soon. She'd probably love your company. The neighbors are all visiting a lot, but she has no family up this way since her husband died, and I think she really misses the rabbits and parakeets.'

'Thank you, ma'am. For doing this for her. I'll let her know what a great job you're doing on the cleaning, too.' I took the map from the car, and she pointed out where the hospital was. She watched me go from the doorway, smiling and waving as I backed out of the driveway and headed east for the hospital.

I looked around. I was amazed at how one hospital room was much like another. Consuelo looked small and tired in her bed. She was breathing heavily and unsteadily through her mouth. An oxygen tube in her nose aided her.

195

I entered the room slowly in order not to startle her. I'd brought with me a teddy bear and a potted plant I'd got in the gift shop on the ground floor of the building. I asked her, 'How are you?' and 'What do the doctors say?' and 'When can you go home?' She started the real conversation, with no prompting from me. I felt bad—I hadn't wanted her to speak, to think or to feel, just to rest. But the minute she'd seen me, she'd known that I knew and that I'd come for her.

'I gave him to her. He was five. I knew that she would love him. I knew he would get the best. He would be a business man ... he would not be like me.'

'But he didn't become any of those things, Consuelo. Oh, never mind ... We can see everything in hindsight, can't we?'

'Sometimes you can look forward, too, if you look carefully. If you ask carefully.' She adjusted her head on her pillow, trying to get a better angle to see me. 'Are you angry at me? Do you think less of me?'

'No.' She accepted this without further question. I decided I should probably elaborate, 'Maybe I would have done the same. It's kind of like sending your kid to boarding school. I just don't know why you haven't seen Dad again.'

'Timing—he left Cuba and I stayed. I left eventually, but not until 1980. It was too long then, I thought. Too much time had passed. I had become a rebel, a member of the party. He had become part of the bourgeoisie, the non-believers. I would not help him by visiting him. I just came here to Lakeland with Miguel and made my new life.'

'Why did you leave?'

'The Revolution ... the Revolution ... because of what happen' to the Revolution, and to all of us. It didn't work out the way we thought it would. Nothing ever does. I suppose. Eventually, I left the party. I left the work I was doing. People were being jailed, people I knew. I denounce' everything and we were treated like dogs on the marina in Mariel. We trusted too much. We loved too much.'

'You loved too much.'

She smiled, 'I loved too much, yes, you are right. I love you, you lovely thing, my blood.' Her eyes looked watery and slightly unfocused. There was a light blue film of cataract on one of them.

'When did Miguel pass away, Consuelo? I wish I'd known him.'

'Ai—years ago, in the eighties. He didn' last. Rubén Castro broke his heart. His body came here, but his soul was in Cuba, hovering above Havana, surveying the cane fields, looking for his mother. You can no live like that. Doctors say it was cancer, but I know the truth.'

I wanted to believe her.

'I have been waiting for you many years. I knew you would come to me. Elegua promised it.'

After everything, Consuelo believed. She believed in her orishas, she believed in all the saints and Jesus Christ and the Virgin Mary. She believed in Marx and Engels and Castro and Khrushchev. She believed in John F. Kennedy and free love and the freedom of speech. She said she'd quit the party, but I knew that some kernel of her still believed, still thought she could have made it work, if only she'd done X differently, if only she'd done Y differently. I'd never known anybody who could believe and who could love like Consuelo could believe and love—with intensity and passion and abandon.

I wanted it. I wanted to have her intensity, her passion. I wanted to love like that. Care like that. I loved in measured drips, with restraint, with reserve. I loved truly, I held on to love and kept it with me for years, but there were no dizzying heights and miserable lows. There were no moments of abandon and experimentation. There was just this mellow steadiness, this attempt at forever. 'I must have gotten this from my mother's side,' I thought.

I looked out the window to the parking lot, sun blistering the sky, nurses walking to their cars at the end of their shifts. We sat in silence for a while, Consuelo not looking directly at me, but me looking at her, trying to see myself in her. My skin was lighter than hers. I had her dark eyes, though— same slant. I had her nose and her height—both small. And I think, maybe, I had just some of her sense of adventure.

'Well, here I am, Consuelo. Elegua was right.'

'He was right again. He never tell me wrong. Do you believe in that? In religion?'

'No. I don't believe in anything anymore.'

'That is wrong. You should believe. It will help you in life.'

I just smiled.

'Is time for my show.' Consuelo turned on an afternoon soap opera. She watched the characters move through their charades of drama and pain and glamor and love.

'You don't need to watch that stuff,' I said. 'Just remember. You have your own form of entertainment in your head.'

'Sometime I don' want to remember. Anyway, I can look at these people and know that I am not alone.'

'No, you're not, Abuela.'

I stayed in Lakeland until the funeral. I was her only blood relation there.

Nosotros No Debemos Olvidar

ortunately, I backup my work regularly. I learned that in college, when I was halfway through a term. I was taking a fiction-writing class as an elective, in addition to the other staples that were required of me that semester: history of the French Revolution, an investigative journalism class, media studies. We had to produce about seventy pages. I was using a small computer popular at the time, a sort of glorified typewriter with a screen. I came home one rainy, cold Northern evening after classes to sit at my desk and add to the forty pages I already had—and it was gone. The machine had died and had taken my work with it. I had to redo everything I had done in the first couple of months of the semester. It was heartbreaking, maddening.

So, when my computer went again during the writing of this, I was prepared. I'd backed it up on diskettes, and I had a hard copy—scribbled on and dog-eared, but legible nonetheless. I'm finishing this manuscript now on an old typewriter. One Abuela Josefina and Abuelo Rogelio gave me for Christmas when I was about nine, I think. It was the biggest thing under there, wrapped in red paper. When I opened it, I didn't know what to think. It looked interesting, but it wasn't a toy, it wasn't clothing, I couldn't ride it, I couldn't take it to school very easily, and I couldn't share it with my friends when I was using it. It was this strange new object, which I could only play with by myself, and which would record anything I typed into it.

On the 26th of December I was taken out to the shops and I bought some onion-skin paper. By that evening I had a story, tapped out, slowly, with one finger. I'd messed the paper up several times, scrunching it in the roller as I tried to get it to go in, smudging the ink, dropping orange juice on the keys. But eventually, I'd gotten it done: a story.

And now here I am with it again. I had to go to my parents' house and into my bedroom, the one I used when I visited home from college, the one I slept in when Josefina died. I dug into the closet on my hands and knees, only my rear end sticking out, digging through shoes, dolls, dusty books and papers, and under everything, at the back, was the small plastic typewriter.

I'm sitting on my bed now, the bed I slept in when I was seventeen, eighteen, nineteen, twenty, twenty-four … I'm tapping away at the keys. They are really small—made for a child's hands. I can't believe the ribbon on this thing is still any good at all. It's another intact memory. There are not many things from the past that you can reach out and touch. I can't reach out to hug Abuela Josefina, or Consuelo.

For work, I cover the Southwest section, the place where I grew up. La Sowesera. There are Guatemalans here now, and Ecuadorians, and Salvadorians and Columbians, Costa Ricans, Hondurans and Peruvians. We are not alone anymore, we Cubans. And these new folk—their children, I can see it in their eyes: they will go on the same journey I went on, that Sara went on, that Rosa went on—that we go on, that never ends. Soon, the whole place will be a United Nations of the walking dead—their bodies wandering the streets of North America, occupying desk chairs, standing behind counters, holding small babies in their hands; but their spirits will be roaming the beaches of Columbia, through the back streets of Guayaquil, the jungles of Guatemala or Costa Rica, touching the pampas grass in Argentina, climbing the mountains of Peru. They will dig and search, and at the end of their journey, they will find themselves in a small bedroom, in La Sowesera, sitting on a faded orange bedspread, with a closet full of clothes that they can no longer fit into in front of them, typing.

GLOSSARY

AI NO JODES	Oh, don't fuck around.
ASÍ MISMO	Just like that.
BIAGUE	Coconut shell oracle, a means of divination that asks for guidance from the gods.
BOCADITO	Little sandwich, a snack food.
BOHÍO	Peasant hut, usually made with palm fronds and having a dirt floor.
CALDO GALLEGO	Galician soup.
CAMPESINO	Country person/peasant.
CANGREJITOS	Little crab shaped pastries, usually filled with meat.
CARNE ASADA	Cuban pot roast.
CHANGO (SHANGO)	An orisha. Originally the fourth king of the Yoruba, also known as the thunder god. Brings a 'purifying moral terror' (Nuñez).
COLÁDA	Large espresso-style coffee.
COMPAÑERA	Comrade (female).
DULCE DE LECHE	A semi-hardened sweet made from milk and sugar.
ELEGUA	An orisha. Elegua is the messenger between humans and the other gods and the first to be honored in any ceremony.
GALLETAS	Crackers.
GRANIZADOS	Shaved ice covered in flavored syrup.

GUAYAVERAS	Typical Cuban short-sleeved shirt for men, worn outside the trousers and made of linen.
GUAJIRO/A	Peasant.
GUARAPO	Sugar-cane juice—great with ice!
HELADITOS	Little ice creams.
HIJÍTA	Little daughter (term of endearment).
LUCUMI	Originally the language of Yoruba slaves, it developed into a particular Cuban language, now used as the sacred language of Santeria worship.
MISERICORDIA	Mercy or compassion.
OBATALA	Creator of men; owner of the world. Invoked for health, peace, harmony. His/her color is white.
OBINÚ	Coconut shell pieces used in coconut oracle divination.
ORISHA	Lower god in pantheon of Santeria. All orishas are subordinate to a supreme being (God), sometimes called Olorun or Oloddumare.
OYEKUN	One of five possible outcomes of consulting the coconut oracle. The meaning is death, but this can be interpreted in a variety of manners.
PASTELLITO DE GUAYAVA	Guava pastry.
POQUÍTO	A little.
PRECARISTAS	Peasant squatters, these were some of the poorest Cubans. They would find a remote part of a landowner's holding to raise a small hut and grow food or hunt. One of the tasks of the mayorales (over-

seers) was to chase them off the land.

SANTERIA	Afro-Cuban religion incorporating elements of traditional West African as well as Roman Catholic beliefs, rituals and deities. The belief system is present in other Caribbean and Latin American countries by other names (Candomble in Brazil, Voodoo in Haiti, etc.).
SANTERO/A	Priest/priestess in the religion of Santeria.
SARACEO	Sacred mixture of toasted corn, smoked fish, corojo (tropical palm) butter, honey, and powdered eggshell.
TASAJO	Jerked beef stew. Now eaten by most Cubans, in the past jerked beef was a common daily ration for slaves.

CHAPTER TITLES

The chapter titles are taken from 'The Hymn of the 26 July' by Agustin Díaz Cartaya:

Marchamos vamos **hacia un ideal**
Sabiendo que vamos a triunfar
Además de paz y prosperidad
Lucharemos todos para la libertad.

Adelante Cubanos!
Que Cuba **premiara nuestro heroismo.**
Pues somos soldados
Que vamos a la Patria a liberar

Limpiando con fuego
Que arrase con esa plaga infernal
De gobernantes indeseables
Y de Tiranos insaciables
Que a Cuba han sumido en el mal.

La sangre que **en Cuba se derramó**
Nosotros no debemos olvidar
Por eso **unidos debemos estar**
Recordando a aquellos
Que muertos están.

El pueblo de Cuba
Sumido en su dolor se siente herido
Y se ha decidido
A hallar sin tregua uni solución
Que sirva de ejemplo
A **esos que no tienen compasión**
Y arriesguemos decididos
Por esta causa dar la vida:
Que viva la Revolución!

Marching **towards an ideal**
Knowing very well we are going to win
More than peace and prosperity
We will all fight for liberty.

Onwards Cubans!
Let Cuba give us **a prize for heroism.**
For we are soldiers
Going to free the country

Cleansing with fire
Which will destroy this infernal plague
Of bad governments
And insatiable tyrants
Who have plunged Cuba into evil.

The blood which **flowed in Cuba**
We must never forget
For that reason we must **stay united**
In remembrance of those
Who died.

The Cuban people
Drowned in grief feel themselves wounded
And have decided
To pursue without respite a solution
Which will **serve as an example**
To **those who don't have pity**
And we risk, resolved
For this cause to give our life:
Long live the Revolution!

REFERENCES

Note that, for the sake of poetic justice, I have taken the liberty of applying the '26th of July Movement' name to the labor camp that Josefina worked in. The 26th of July Movement camp was in Esmerelda in Camagüey province, and did not necessarily engage in sugar-cane farming.

García, María Cristina, *Havana USA: Cuban Exiles and Cuban Americans in South Florida, 1959–1994* (University of California Press, Berkeley and Los Angeles 1996).

Hugh, Thomas, *Cuba or the Pursuit of Freedom* (Picador Press, New York 1971).

http://cuban-exile.com/

'Informe sobre la situacíon de los derechos humanos en Cuba', Country Report: Cuba, OEA/SER.L/V/II.17, Doc. 4 (Español), 7 de Abril 1967. Published by the Organization of American States. www.cidh.oas.org

Nuñez, Luis M., *Santeria, A Practical Guide to Afro-Caribbean Magic* (Spring Publications Inc., Putnam, Connecticut 1992).

World Circuit Music Publishing.

ACKNOWLEDGMENTS

Thanks to: Mom for believing; Dad for the Stories; Brendan for everything; Berta Mont-Ros and Helaine Chiger for unfailing support; Beth Herstein for useful comments and great insight; Mark Mirsky of CUNY; and of course everyone at Sitric, including Antony Farrell, Kathy Gilfillan, Sarah Liddy and Marsha Swan.